TUMBLEWEED TRAIL

**Center Point
Large Print**

**This Large Print Book carries the
Seal of Approval of N.A.V.H.**

LAURAN PAINE

TUMBLEWEED TRAIL

CENTER POINT PUBLISHING
THORNDIKE, MAINE • USA

BOLINDA PUBLISHING
MELBOURNE • AUSTRALIA

This Center Point Large Print edition is published in the year 2003 by arrangement with Golden West Literary Agency.

This Bolinda Large Print edition is published in the year 2003 by arrangement with Center Point Publishing.

The text of this Large Print edition is unabridged. In other aspects, this book may vary from the original edition. Printed in Thailand. Set in 16-point Times New Roman type by Bill Coskrey and Gary Socquet.

US ISBN 1-58547-293-X
BC ISBN 1-74030-942-1

U.S. Library of Congress Cataloging-in-Publication Data.

Paine, Lauran.
    Tumbleweed trail / Lauran Paine.--Center Point large print ed.
      p. cm.
    Originally published in England under the name: Russ Thompson.
    ISBN 1-58547-293-X (lib. bdg. : alk. paper)
     1. Large type books. I. Title.

PS3566.A34 T8 2003
813'.54--dc21

                  2002035123

Australian Cataloguing-in-Publication.

Paine, Lauran.
Tumbleweed trail / Lauran Paine.
ISBN 1740309421
1. Large print books.
2. Western stories.
I. Title.
813.6

British Cataloguing-in-Publication is available from the British Library.

ONE

F ROM the divide northward lay a flowing emptiness which ran out to the far merging of sky and earth. Bitterbrush Basin it was called, and it lay between the Moccasin Mountains to the north and the Tumbleweed Mountains to the south.

In springtime cattlemen from farther south pushed their drives over into Bitterbrush Basin, but excepting a few scruffy Piute Indians no one lived in the Bitterbrush country. For one thing it was so huge and empty, so treeless and flinty-soiled, that no cowman had ever even tried to claim its worthless land. For another thing, in wintertime wind storms shrieking down from the Moccasin Mountains turned it into a howling waste with alkali dust so thick it choked a man and burned his eyes.

But each spring when the bunch-grass came, Bitterbrush Basin saw the cattle drives, some heading in from the west, a few from the east, but mostly the trail-drives came up through Tumbleweed Pass where wind-shaped old sandstone spires stood eternal watch; then Bitterbrush Basin, for a brief time, had men in it.

That short-stemmed bunch-grass was strong and full of nutrition. It grew in the lee of the stunted sage, at the base of the sumac, and around every bitterbrush clump.

From the divide above Tumbleweed Pass though, a man could sit his saddle and look backwards into the

Basin and view such emptiness, such desolation, as few men ever saw in their lifetimes, and if he was not a seasoned rider he might wonder why any cowman in his right mind would make the drive into that place at all, for from the top of the Tumbleweeds you couldn't see that short-stemmed, good grass, all you saw was a thousand miles of alkali dust and emptiness.

But southward, out a few miles from the Tumbleweeds, there was a patch of green where a dun-brown fold in the low hills held a promise of water. In that fold also, were quaking aspens and cottonwoods, sure-fire indicators of water. In fact, the farther southward a rider travelled the better Nevada became, until, below the Humboldt Sink lay the extravagant greenery of California.

But that was a long ride, and to anyone passing down-country from the Moccasins across Bitterbrush Basin and up into the sandstone reaches of the wind-smoothed old Tumbleweed Mountains, the unexpectedness of that inviting place down below and out a little ways where the aspen trees grew, was a sight to make a rider pause.

Tumbleweed Pass lay west a half mile of the top-out where one first sighted that patch of welcome green in the otherwise dreary Nevada landscape, and to the people who lived southward of the Tumbleweeds there was a knowing way of looking at a man who said he'd arrived in the country by way of that Pass.

No one who knew better ever came out of the settled north into the desolation of Nevada by way of Moccasin Mountains. Unless, as the cowmen of the south country said, he was in an almighty hurry to leave civilisation behind. They called that north-to-south passage the Tumbleweed Trail, meaning that the rare few riders who came down from the north that way, were like tumbleweeds; they were footloose, the winds of trouble blew them one way then another way. Like the tumbleweeds themselves, which bounced and rolled and tumbled end over end with every shifting wind of fall and winter, those strangers drifted along ahead of the wind. Time and experience had proved the cattlemen to be correct about this. Not many riders came down the Tumbleweed Trail, but when they did, when a cowman spied a solitary horseman passing along through Bitterbrush Basin, if the cowman had any sense he casually turned his horse and looked the other way. He did not under any circumstances, ride over to intercept the stranger. Men had been killed doing that. The Tumbleweed Trail might be an invisible passage, but it was nonetheless very real to the sparse inhabitants of the south country.

But no one saw that pre-dawn rider for the elemental fact that, aside from his night passage across the Basin, it was still a month early for the cattle drives to be heading northward into the Basin, so he sat his saddle atop the Tumbleweeds, a half mile east of the Pass, and let new sunlight build up its steady early-spring warmth along his right side, while he studied the onward fold in the sage-brush hills where those aspen and cottonwoods grew.

He told his horse in a soft-drawling voice that there would be grass down in that draw, and maybe even a red-plum thicket beside a creek—if they were lucky. What he did not tell his horse because he could not see it, was that a weathered house and barn were also down in that draw.

If he'd stayed atop the ridge long enough, when the sun got a little higher it would have grittily shone off two tin roofs down there. But he turned the big bay horse, edged along to a buck-run and angled on down into the sandstone dust of Tumbleweed Pass, outward bound straight towards those welcome trees.

He had progressed close to a mile when a thin, angry cry rang out off to his left a short distance, where dawn sunlight hadn't quite obliterated night-time's last smoky haze. The man lifted his reins with his left hand, drooped his right hand close to the holstered .45 lashed to his right leg, and sat like stone for as long as it took him to block-in a big chunk of that emptiness where the shout had come from. For a long while he saw nothing. Overhead, up along the barren Tumble-weed ridge, pink sunlight softly shone, but lower down where the duskiness lay, the world was as it must have been since the world's beginning.

Then a short-horned brindle cow came awkwardly lumbering into sight stepping left and right through the stunted brush, and the horseman sighted it at once. So did his big bay horse, rangy and long-legged, sloping-rumped, leaned down to rawhide toughness from much riding. The horse pointed little ears, turning very interested. This was the first animal except for one band of racing antelope it had seen in two days.

The cow came on in her ungainly run, head up and tail straight out. She had a big swollen bag which impeded her progress but she never slowed until she saw the horse and rider athwart her trail. With a big snort she slammed down to a stiff-legged halt, rattled her horns and struck up a cloud of dust with one pawing forefoot.

The horseman smiled. She was someone's milk cow. Making those threatening gestures with horns and hoof were instinctive rather than dangerous. For a full minute the man and milk cow studied one another. The cow could easily have walked on around the man, but obviously his appearance in this empty world had so startled her, had so aroused her curiosity, that she seemed not to think of going on around him.

A little wisp of movement farther back caught the man's attention. He moved his eyes a fraction and sighted the boy coming furiously along on the old cow's trail. The lad was lanky and walked with a thrusting stride. He had a long switch in one hand and a cotton length of rope in the other hand.

He was on foot and seemed for that reason to be entirely out of place in this vast emptiness. He was hatless too, and wore no jacket, only an old faded hickory shirt and faded levis. To the man these things all added up to a ranch somewhere hereabouts. But he had only a moment to speculate on these things. The old cow heard the boy coming and wrung her tail, swung to peer backwards, then started moving again.

The lad looked up, saw the cow, and probably because the man was perfectly motionless, did not see him at all. He called out in a reedy, angry voice, hurled a sizzling epithet at the old cow. Then he spied the rider sitting there and stopped dead-still. He was not so far off the man didn't see his eyes suddenly spring wide and his face abruptly lose all its anger, becoming at once watchful and woodenly blank.

The man took down his lariat, built a little loop and as though in perfect understanding his big bay horse pranced sideways towards the cow. She stopped, switched her tail at sight of that loop, ducked her horns in that threatening way again, and as her head came back up the loop settled evenly down over her head. She was no novice at this game; as soon as the slack drew up, all her earlier resistance atrophied. She stood quietly waiting for whatever came next, and steadily watching the man.

That lanky lad made no move to approach any closer than he already was. In fact he seemed to the man to be poised to whip around and race away, so the man called over to him.

"Come get her. She's got her run out now."

The boy started obediently forward with his lead-rope and his switch, and although he caustically eyed the cow from time to time, his main interest was in that man atop the big bay horse. When he was within twenty feet of the cow and under the calm gaze of the man, he said, obviously feeling that he had to say something, "She takes one of those playful spells every once in a while."

"Yeah," agreed the man, with a little bob of his head. "They all do. Only this one isn't exactly built for running."

The lad eased up, secured his rope and dropped the man's loop. The cow switched her tail and rolled her eyes.

"Better toss away that switch," the man said. "I know how you feel, but bustin' her one'll only make her worse. Odd thing about cow-critters. The madder a feller gets at 'em the crazier they become. That's one of the sorry things about bein' a two-legged animal; you got to show more sense than critters got, even when you're mad enough to shoot 'em. I reckon if a man couldn't do that he wouldn't be any smarter'n the animal, would he?"

The lanky youth shook his head. He was considering the man with less scepticism now and more plain curiosity. As he put up a hand to scratch the old cow he said, "Mister; did you just come down through that Pass yonder?"

"Yep. And across the big basin before I got to the Pass." The man drew in his lariat and quietly coiled it. "Darned sorry hunk of world back there," he observed, strapping the rope into place on the right side of his saddle-fork.

"It's called Bitterbrush Basin, mister. That Pass is called Tumbleweed Pass. Those mountains are the

11

Tumbleweeds. I guess you never been through here before."

The rider put a thoughtful gaze forward and down-ward. He was a sun-layered man in his late twenties or early thirties. His gaze was like oak-smoke on a wintry day. He was solidly built and slab-hammed. He looked hard as rock and about as durable. He also looked very wise in the ways of other people, so he sat up there regarding the boy for a moment before he spoke, and then his voice was dry and knowing.

"Nope; never been through here before," he said, "and I'm gettin' a feeling that's against me."

The boy reddened, dropped his eyes to the old cow and shifted his footing. "Not exactly," he said defen-sively, then lapsed into awkward silence because he didn't know what else to say. If he told the stranger the truth—what folks said concerning strangers who came down the Tumbleweed Trail—it not only wouldn't be polite, it just might also be dangerous.

The man's steely grey eyes lay quietly upon the boy for another little interval of thoughtful silence, then he said, "Tell me, pardner; do you live around here some-where?"

The lad turned, lifted an arm and pointed over into that draw where the aspen and cottonwoods were. "The buildings are up there in the trees," he said, "and we own all the land for five miles around. Right up to Tumbleweed Pass, in fact."

The man moved in his saddle and seemed to be dis-appointed about something. Looking up that draw he

12

said, "You got a red-plum thicket up there, pardner?"

"Yes. But they aren't ripe yet."

"Well; you got grass and water up there, haven't you?"

"Sure."

"Well now," said the man, swinging his eyes back again. "You reckon your paw'd sell me a day's grass and water and rest for my horse?"

"My maw sure would," said the boy, shortened his hold on the old cow's lead-shank and half turned. "Come on; I'll show you the way."

TWO

THE man rode along keen-eyed and interested behind the lad and his cow. At first there was no trail to follow but when the swale came closer several trails appeared. The man studied these all the way into the draw, then he saw the ranch house, the tin-roofed barn and the several nondescript out-buildings seemingly put down without much thought where the cottonwood trees were thickest.

It dawned upon the man that whoever had put these buildings back in here did not just accidentally do this. Unless a rider knew the buildings were there, shaded but also secreted among those trees, he could ride within a hundred yards of them and not spot them at all.

The house was low and long and solid. The barn was sturdily made of logs, probably hauled at considerable cost and sweat, from the miles-away mountains west-erly or southerly, for there was no timber worthy of the name in either the Moccasins or the Tumbleweeds.

The lad led his old cow into the barn, poked his head back out to watch the stranger dismount and tie his horse, twist slowly to put a long, careful look out and around, then hike on over where the door was being held open for him.

But the man did not enter; he instead stood in that opened doorway alternately talking to the lad, where he squatted under his old cow, and keeping his watch of the countryside.

The lanky, shockle-headed youth was thirteen years old, but he'd grown up in this hushed, half-expectant, half-curious environment, so as he watched the stranger stand over there he said, "Mister; doesn't anyone ever come around here. Maybe once or twice a year the cowboys drop by on their way into the basin or out of it, but aside from that only Shelton Leonard ever comes by."

"Shelton Leonard?" asked the man.

"Yeah. He owns a place west of us a few miles. He comes over about once a week."

The man listened to this, dismissed it and said, "Where's your closest town?"

"Well; couple times a year we hitch up and drive over to Bidwell. That's sixty miles off." The boy stopped milking long enough to lift an arm and point across the range south-eastward. As he resumed milking he said, "But it's too far off for visitin' and

14

stuff like that."

The man suddenly stiffened where he stood. From around the barn came soft footfalls. The boy did not hear them until the man loosened again, so when he gazed upwards the man seemed as loose and easy-standing as before. Those footfalls were light and close-spaced. The footfalls of a woman.

"In here," bawled the lad, and in the same loud tone of voice began explaining to the unseen but approaching woman what had taken him so long.

She came smoothly around the barn's rough log corner, saw the gun-belted stranger standing there gazing steadily down at her, and stopped dead-still with her violet eyes instantly widening and her face turning abruptly pale.

She was an unusually striking woman, tall and willowy, which seemed to be where the boy had gotten that lankiness of his, and her tawny reddish hair was thick and heavily looped in soft-shining waves.

Her mouth was long with a little upward lilt at its outer corners. The lips were heavy and inviting. Her eyes were deepest blue and now, with colour gone from her cheeks, they seemed enormous.

She didn't possibly seem old enough to be the mother of that garrulously talking boy inside the barn which neither she nor the man were now heeding, and yet, there were the unmistakable similarities, not just in the height but also in the hair-colour, the mouth, and the quick expression of withdrawn wariness both showed when surprised.

"I'm Sloan Verrill," the man quietly said, and removed his hat. "I met your boy out chasing the cow."

She kept watching him, but after that first shock at finding a total stranger leaning there in her barn doorway, those violet eyes turned sceptical, turned wondering and doubtful about him. He could feel the wall come between them.

She stepped over and peered into the barn, saw the boy industriously juicing that old cow, then she put a cool look upwards at the man. "Is there something you want here, Mister Verrill?" she asked.

"Yes'm; I'd like to buy a day's grass and rest for my horse."

She swung to consider Verrill's highly-bred horse with its built-in capacity for great speed and great endurance. Her gaze was sombre. She almost said something about the bay horse but in the end she didn't, she simply walked back down to the edge of the barn, stopped there looking downward for a moment, then turned back.

"There won't be any charge, Mister Verrill. But you'll leave tomorrow, won't you?"

"Yes'm," he said, feeling that wall between them become quite solid and unscalable.

She kept watching him from an impassively handsome face. She seemed to be comparing him to something or to someone. Abruptly she said, "Breakfast in ten minutes, Mister Verrill," and went on out of sight back around the barn.

Verrill raised his hat, dropped it upon the back of his head, pursed his lips and blew out a long breath. He had, in his lifetime, run across his share of women, friendly and unfriendly, but he couldn't right now recall ever seeing one as naturally handsome in a wild setting as this one, nor as courteously cold and aloof.

The lad emerged from the barn with his bucket of milk. He looked southward as though expecting his mother to still be there, and when he saw that she was not he shrugged. "Come on; I'll show you where the little pasture is. You can turn your horse out."

They passed along to a patched, sagging gate between two stalwart cottonwoods. Here, Verrill off-saddled, hung his outfit from a low limb by one stirrup, and led the bay horse on through. The grass was rank in this shady, sub-irrigated place. The horse walked twenty feet out, folded his front legs and went down. He rolled over and back and blissfully grunted. Then he got up, sniffed the air and went walking off.

"Smells our horses," said the boy. "We got a team and one saddle animal." The lad picked up his bucket, still watching Verrill's sleek, big breedy horse. "But they aren't like your horse, mister. They're old."

Verrill put a hand upon the lad's arm detaining him. "You better call me Sloan," he said. "It sounds better than mister." Verrill pushed out that same detaining hand and waited.

The boy looked up into Verrill's face with the same deep blue eyes his mother had. He seemed unsure and suddenly self-conscious. He put down the bucket, manfully shook Verrill's hand and said, "I'm Trent Drummond. You already met my mother; her name's Rita. Rita Drummond."

"And your paw, Trent; when'll I meet him?"

Trent reached for the bucket, lifted it and without a word turned and started away from the house back up through the cottonwoods. He kept moving in and out of tree-shade until, upon a little grassy slope up where the quaking aspens grew he halted. There was a paling-fence in this sun-bright spot and a lone aspen grew inside the fence.

"There," the lad solemnly said, pointing to the weathered headboard above a slightly sunken place. "That's where my paw's buried."

From downhill and through the trees a bell clanged. Young Trent Drummond roused himself, turned and without another word or glance started on towards the house. Sloan Verrill walked thoughtfully along behind him.

The sun was fully up now, dazzling golden light lay everywhere except in among those ancient cotton-woods. A good warmth took the dawn-edge off the early morning and there was a sage-fragrance in the air. At the rear of the ranch house stood the outside washstand. Here, young Trent halted and stood back until Verrill had cleaned up, then he drew a fresh pan of wash-water from the pump, made puppyish sounds as he also washed, and afterwards the pair of them walked on into the large, immaculate kitchen.

Rita Drummond threw a quick, careful look over at

Verrill when he stepped through the doorway. Trent packed his milk bucket over and set it in the sink. He then mechanically levered the pump filling the sink with cold water to cool-out that lukewarm milk and detachedly began telling his mother once more how the cow had tried to run off.

"Mister Verrill roped her neat as whistle," he said in conclusion, and turned to grin over where those two silent adults were awkwardly considering one another. "I sure didn't expect to see him sittin' his horse there, though. Sure startled me, Ma."

Rita Drummond, her eyes upon Verrill, said softly, "I can imagine, son. Now you'd better eat."

As Trent dutifully crossed over to the laden breakfast table he said in the half-careless, half-observant way of boys, "Maw; did you see Sloan's horse? He's sure built to run, isn't he? Remember when paw's horse, old Bally, looked like that?"

Rita Drummond had her back to them over at the cook-stove. She said, "Yes, I remember when Bally was like that, son." She was busy over there frying meat and potatoes for a moment before she also said, "They're all like that, when they come riding down the Tumbleweed Trail, Trent."

Verrill, in the act of sitting down, caught the undertone, the soft bitterness, in those words. He eased on down and sat thoughtful for a moment before he said, "Ma'm; a trail is a trail."

Trent started eating. He sensed nothing here and anyway he was hungry. Walking a mile after a recalcitrant milk cow made a person hungry.

From the stove Rita Drummond turned to bring over the potato platter. She did not look at Verrill but she said, "Some trails get more travel than others, Mister Verrill."

He kept watching her. She was a very handsome woman. Her figure was full and solid, her wealth of softly curled hair framed her face, especially her heavy mouth and those dead-level violet eyes. When she came within ten feet of him a quickening current of some kind sang out along his nerves.

He said, "There are all kinds of people in this world so there have to also be all kinds of trails."

She still avoided his gaze, nor did she pursue this conversation. Instead, as she seated herself across from Verrill she said to Trent, "Maybe today we could go up and fix the dam."

Trent bobbed his head wordlessly up and down. He stowed away a lot of breakfast and he afterwards leaned back to put a boyishly interested look upon Sloan Verrill's powerful arms, chest and shoulders, and say, "Maybe Sloan'd help us with the logs, maw."

His mother said nothing. She was still sedulously avoiding Verrill's gaze. Trent though, still failed to notice any undercurrent here. He launched into an explanation of what his mother had meant about fixing the dam.

"Up the draw a mile we got a log dam across the creek to lift the water an' put it into our irrigation ditches. That's how we keep the grass green down here. But the danged beavers keep gnawin' up our logs an' right now most of the water's going through breaks in the dam so doesn't very much get into the ditches any more."

Sloan finished eating and smiled. "I reckon you an' I could take care of that without troublin' your mother," he said, pushed back his chair and stood up. His solid, powerful frame dwarfed the others in that room. His low-slung, tied-down six-gun with its walnut stock made a graceful silhouette as he reached down, scooped up his hat and straightened around towards Rita Drummond. "No point in you comin' along, ma'm," he said quietly, and jerked his head at young Trent.

Those two walked back on out into the piling-up heat. Verrill had a little puckered frown drawing his dark brows inward as he thoughtfully put his hat on. It faded as Trent said, boyishly enthusiastic, "Come on; the shovels and crow-bars are in the tool shed."

Armed with their tools those two went walking westward on up beside the little clear-water creek, Trent leading, Sloan Verrill following. All the way up to the log dam Trent talked. He skipped blithely from one topic to another seemingly delighted to have a man to talk to. Without perhaps meaning to he told Verrill many things; how long his parents had been here, how his mother taught him letters and numbers by the fireplace at night, how the cattlemen sometimes came by, all the little inconsequential things which were of importance to a thirteen-year-old boy.

The man listened and said nothing. In fact he scarcely heard, or at least seemed to hear, much of what Trent said. He was privately fitting the things Rita Drummond had said into a logical pattern. What he came up with when he totalled all those remarks, and those distant, sceptical looks, made a picture he found interesting. But he mentioned none of this to the boy.

Then they arrived up where someone had long before built a cleverly engineered dam. Leading outward and southward from this place were the little feeder-ditches which carried water down to the green places.

Trent grounded his tools, pointed triumphantly to a boiling rush of water, and said, "Danged beavers anyway. I never could figure out how they come to find this creek. This sure isn't beaver country, Sloan. Too dry an' hot most of the time."

Sloan considered the heaped-up pile of limbs, leaves and brush, plastered over with mud which constituted a beaver's home, and sighed. They would be working in water above their knees. He sat down and began tugging off his boots.

"You better do the same," he told Trent, "and roll up your pants too. That water's goin' to be almighty cold."

When Sloan stepped forth gingerly into the icy creek water using a crow-bar to steady himself, young Trent looked over and said, "You better shed your gun too. It might get wet, out there."

Sloan paused, twisted and gazed steadily at Trent. "Roll those pants up, pardner," he said, completely ignoring Trent's admonition about his six-gun. "This water's colder'n an Indian's heart."

Trent fixed his trouser-legs, walked over and stepped boldly down into the water. He laughed. It was a musical, rich sound that seemed to somehow merge with the equally as musical sound of the rushing little creek.

"When it gets hot, later on, I come up here an' swim behind the dam."

Sloan got out where the beaver dam was, heaved his crow-bar into the interlaced limbs and trash, leaned a moment studying the best way to demolish this thing so that they could afterwards get to the gnawed places in the logs, and said, "Oak logs would last longer than these cottonwoods. Are there any oaks around?"

"Over on the Leonard place there are," answered Trent, working his way closer to Sloan. "But maw says we aren't to ask Shelton Leonard for anything."

Verrill slowly turned and slowly gazed at young Trent. To a thoughtful man accustomed to reading meaning where it was not intentionally offered, the lad's statement was chock-full of significance.

"Well," Sloan said, leaning on his crow-bar, "let's get to work. I got nothin' much against water, but when it's this cold I can sure think of a lot of other places I'd rather be standin'."

THREE

THEY got the trash clear of those gnawed logs and climbed out to sit upon the warm earth considering what must be done next. "The trouble is," stated young Trent with a furrowed brow and resentful eyes, "those danged beavers will come back and make another home and chew holes in the logs again."

Sloan removed his hat, tossed it aside and gazed quietly around this peaceful, pleasantly sunlighted place. He idly said, "You got a couple of pieces of that roof-tin in the barn?"

Trent's face brightened instantly. He looked admiringly over where Sloan was lying propped on one elbow. "Now why didn't I think of that, for gosh sakes? Sure; I'll go fetch us a couple of pieces after while. And some nails too. The doggoned critters can't gnaw through tin, can they?"

Sloan, with his body lying all loose against the ground, shook his head and considered the boy from pensive eyes. The ancient ways of youth never changed; there was enthusiasm and bubbling conversation. There was also, deeply lost in a young boy's mind, all the little things which were dormant at thirteen, but which in later years would show the rough edges of character, sometimes good, sometimes bad. The trouble was, unless a man had watched a lad grow, he never really knew what kind of a man would some day emerge.

"Sloan?"

"Yeah."

"Have you fixed log dams before?"

"I reckon everyone's fixed log dams sometime, Trent."

"In Nevada?"

Sloan's reply to this came slowly and only after a little quiet interval. " 'You fishing?" he asked.

Trent blushed violently; he had indeed been fishing, and in the only world young Trent Drummond had ever known, it was a serious breach of etiquette to pry into the past of others. Trent jumped up and reached for his shovel. "I'll go clean out the rest of that trash behind the dam," he said quickly, and started away.

"Trent?"

The boy turned, gazing straight over at the man.

"In Utah, not Nevada."

Sloan rose up, reached for his crow-bar and ambled over. He viewed their work thus far and without looking down or around he said, "Tell you what; you go fetch the tin and nails. I'll finish cleaning out behind the dam. All right?"

"All right."

After Trent had darted off down the creek, the sturdily-built man gazed after him and slowly, gently, smiled. When a man took the long step from his twenties into his thirties boyhood seemed an awfully long way behind him. But still, a man could remember clearly enough, when there was something to remind him. Something like a shockle-headed lanky kid full of candour and forthright honesty.

Sloan stepped back down into the chilly water, muttered a quiet curse and went resolutely ahead to finish cleaning out behind the log dam. He had no idea he was not alone until, straightening around towards the north, he sighted quiet movement among the aspens. He instantly let go of the crow-bar with his right hand and stood looking.

Rita Drummond stepped forth with a basket over one arm. She and Sloan Verrill exchanged a long look before she moved over closer and said to him in her quiet way, "A man always holds a crow-bar in his left hand, doesn't he, Mister Verrill; he always drops his right hand when he's come on to suddenly?"

Sloan studied the handsome woman without answering. When they were alone, without Trent close by to hear, there were no reasons to pretend. Her expression told him that now, so he inclined his head and began edging over towards the bank. When he stepped out of the creek and felt good, warm and mouldy earth underfoot, he said, "Ma'm; it's only for one day. You won't have to keep your guard up after that."

"Riders of the Tumbleweed Trail," she murmured and sadly shook her head at him, her gaze cloudy and troubled.

"I got the inference at the barn, and later, at breakfast. You've made your point. You don't trust me. Well, ma'am, I can't help that."

26

He looked around as Trent came trotting along, his face red and sweat-shiny from exertion. The boy called flutingly ahead to his mother, telling her in a rush of words how Sloan Verrill had come up with the one conceivably sound idea anyone had yet offered, to prevent the beavers from gnawing holes in the dam again. His mother smiled and said, "Wonderful. You two make the patch and I'll spread out some lunch."

Sloan took one sheet of the roofing tin, some nails and a hammer, stepped back down into the water and worked his way over to the dam again. He worked with the sure confidence of a person who invariably found himself in familiar situations. He did not look back where Rita Drummond was spreading a calico tablecloth upon the shady grass and began lifting food from her little wicker hamper, until he was finished. Then he twisted, shot a glance over Trent's head where the lad stood close by with their second sheet of tin, and his gaze met the dead-level stare of Rita Drummond where she had paused to watch. Something quick and vital passed back and forth between those two. Rita faced away and resumed laying out their picnic lunch, her sturdy upper body profiled to Verrill, her coppery hair alight with filtered sunbeams from overhead, through cottonwood branches.

"Hey," Trent said to Sloan. "You got a crick in your neck: Here; I'll put this other sheet into place."

But Sloan took one end of the tin, dropped his head and went silently, briskly to work. It took only another minute to make the second tin sheet secure, and at once water began rising up their legs to show that their patch job was not only completed, but also was satisfactory.

When Trent straightened up to jut his underlip and blow upwards at a low-hanging lock of curly auburn hair, he said triumphantly, "There; now let those danged beavers build another home an' try to chew through for their doorway. They'll get their darned teeth dulled in a hurry."

With more tempered judgment Sloan Verrill, also examining their work, wagged his head. "Tin rusts fast in water, Trent. Maybe next year or the year after you'll have to do this over again, so you'd better make sure there are a couple more sheets of this tin at the barn."

"There are," exclaimed Trent promptly, beginning to splash his way towards shore. He stopped in the shallowest place to peer up where the little ditches were beginning to rapidly fill with backed-up irrigation water. "It didn't work this good even when it was new," he said, referring to the dam. "Come on, Sloan; we can eat now."

But Verrill took his time. He put on his socks, his boots, retrieved their tools and put them handy to the homeward trail. He even picked up his hat from the trampled grass and carefully brushed it.

When he finally turned he found Rita Drummond's eyes on him in a wondering, softly disturbed way. "I'm sorry," she whispered. "I didn't mean to sound— like that. Please come eat with us, Mister Verrill."

"Sloan," exclaimed Trent. "Ma; just call him Sloan. He doesn't like that 'mister' business. And anyway, it sounds sort of. . . ." Trent looked around at Sloan while he reached for a word that eluded him.

"Formal," said his mother, and began filling a plate as Verrill walked on over and sank down cross-legged.

Trent ate as though eating might the very next moment become a lost art. His mother looked reproving but said nothing. Sloan smiled. "Takes a heap of vittles to keep ahead of a growin' boy," he said, looking fully into Rita Drummond's eyes as she handed him his plate. "And some day this one's going to be over six feet tall."

It was very pleasant there beside the brawling little white-water creek with a hot overhead sun's rays filtered downward through silvery-green cottonwood leaves. There were lupins and Indian paintbrush growing along the shadowy hillsides. There were dreary, endless miles of emptiness elsewhere, all around, giving this little private place a secluded drowsiness, an emerald, peaceful atmosphere sufficient to bring a gentleness to the most troubled heart.

After they finished eating Trent dropped back flat down and closed his eyes. He did this with the identical spontaneity with which he did most things. He was as uninhibited as a puppy, and watching him now, Sloan Verrill was wistful for the long-gone time when he'd been the same way.

"Do you have any tobacco?" Rita Drummond suddenly asked.

Sloan looked across at her mildly surprised. When he did not immediately reply she reached deep down into the wicker hamper, brought forth an unopened bag of Bull Durham and offered it to him.

He was not a smoker; at least when he had no tobacco, as now, he neither wished for it nor missed it. Still, he gravely accepted that little sack and ducked his head for as long as it took him to make a smoke and light up.

She didn't smoke, he knew that, and neither did young Trent, so evidently this corn-husk dry Bull Durham had been left over from another time. He thought quietly of that weathered headboard out upon the north slope, and wondered what kind of a man her husband had been. A smoker—but what else had he been?

She was gazing away from him, over where the dammed-up creek water was just beginning to make its thin silvery flow up and over and down the reworked dam. He removed his cigarette also watching that crystal-clear shimmering water.

"Make a mighty fine swimming hole," he said, bringing her attention back to him with that statement.

"Yes. Trent spends most of his hot summertime days up here."

"Lonely though," he said, flicking off ash with one finger. "A boy needs at least a dog, or maybe a fawn, or even a young raccoon."

"He's never had a dog."

"No? No dogs available around here?"

She looked him squarely in the eye. "His father didn't want a dog around."

Sloan said softly, "I see." Those two words told her that he understood; men who hid out in secluded cottonwood canyons sixty miles from a town, eight or ten miles from their nearest neighbour, didn't want a dog yapping every time a rider passed through. Barking dogs might be helpful under some circumstances, but under other circumstances they could prove a genuine menace.

She started gathering up their dishes and cups. He watched her sure, supple movements for a while over the curl of cigarette smoke, wondering how it would be for a woman like her left alone in this hushed and secret place.

She suddenly said, without looking up at him, "When you were his age, Mister Verrill, did you have a dog?"

"Yes'm. I think that dog taught me more than the school marm did. He was a collie as big as a wolf an' when I cried he cried too."

She finished with the cleaning up, rocked back and looked straight at him in that disconcertingly dead-level way of hers. "You don't look like a man who ever cried, Mister Verrill. You seem to be a man who would be at home under any circumstances."

He smoked on, watching sunbeams get snarled in her hair, seeing the hidden strain below the surface of her handsome features. He shrugged. "My father was a fine man, ma'am. He taught me to face life head-on."

"Did he also teach you honour and decency, Mister Verrill?"

"Yes, ma'am," he answered, then pushed right ahead eclipsing whatever she might have ironically said to that. "So, if I came riding along your Tumbleweed Trail, and you branded me with whatever you think I am, my father's not to blame."

"He also taught you truthfulness, didn't he?" she said very softly.

Sloan Verrill got to his feet and reached for the basket. "I'll pack it back to the house for you. Hey, Trent; you sleep all night. During the day a man who sleeps misses the little important lessons of life. Come on; get up."

FOUR

IN early afternoon Trent and Verrill fixed that little sagging gate into the horse pasture. They patched a set of bone-dry leather harness and oiled it. It was while they were doing this, taking the harness apart, piece by piece, dipping it into heated neatsfoot oil mixed with mutton tallow, that Rita Drummond suddenly appeared in the barn doorway to say a little breathlessly: "There's a rider coming."

Verrill wiped his hands, shot Rita a look, then stepped outside and walked out through the trees to an open slope and turned slowly around up there where he had an uninterrupted view until he saw that horseman. He was coming on from the west. Sunlight struck the metal butt of his up-ended Winchester, it was also reflected off the cheek-pieces of a silver-mounted Spanish bit. The man was a long mile out but he was unmistakably heading straight for the Drummond place. He was riding a good chestnut horse, and he sat his saddle straight up, like a man would who has something strongly in mind.

Verrill turned at a rustling in the grass behind him, saw Trent and his mother walking towards him, let some of the wire-tightness go out of his stance and waited for those two to also get a good look at the oncoming rider.

It was Trent who named the rider. "It's Shelton Leonard, Maw, I know that chestnut of his a mile off, and that silvered spade bit he rides."

Verrill lifted his gaze and watched Trent's mother. Her expression became guarded, became uneasy. She didn't say a word, she just stood there watching the horseman come swinging along down the distant slope.

Verrill pondered the forthcoming visitation a while before he said, "Trent; I reckon this isn't any of your affair or mine. Suppose you'n I just step back into the barn and finish oiling the harness."

The boy nodded, but his glance, which had up to now been open and pleasant, became guarded and slightly sullen. He turned to head back towards the barn. So did Sloan Verrill. As he passed Rita Drummond he said softly, "Ma'am; I get the feeling this Shelton Leonard's not too welcome here."

She pulled her gaze away from that approaching rider but she still said nothing. She simply gazed up into Verrill's face.

He said, "Well, ma'am, if you don't care about havin' him around neither do I," and walked on past. She turned slowly to watch Verrill and her son head back down through the trees towards the barn. Her gaze became sardonic; it was not difficult to imagine her thoughts: She was thinking that what Verrill had meant was that he would just as soon Shelton Leonard did not know he was at the ranch. Her heavy mouth turned bitter.

Verrill moved his pan of oil closer to the barn door as he and Trent returned to oiling the harness. He had an excellent view of the yonder house and the intervening yard from there, and he watched. While young Trent talked on ramblingly, Sloan Verrill kept his vigil.

He saw this Leonard character come down the last bitterbrush slope and cross over into the trees ahead of the house. He saw him step down and it seemed that Leonard was a little unsteady in his footing, as though he'd been days in the saddle.

Rita walked forth from around front to halt where Leonard was tying his animal. Her back was to Verrill but Leonard's face was visible past her when he smiled and made a little gallant bow before removing his hat. Leonard was a rawboned, rough-looking tall man who stood over six feet tall and looked heavier than he actually was because of the short-waisted sheepskin rider's coat he wore. He had a swarthy face which was narrow at forehead and chin, a long lantern jaw, and eyes the colour of wet obsidian on either side of a high-bridged, Indian-like nose.

He put Sloan Verrill in mind of a predatory bird with that hawkish face and those long legs. When he smiled, though, Leonard's face was made a little less repelling. His teeth were even, large, and very white. He was smiling now as he said something to Rita Drummond. She shook her head at him. Verrill could hear nothing of what was being said, as much because of the intervening distance as because of the droning of young Trent's voice.

Leonard put his hat back on, thumbed it far back and leaned upon the hitchrack, his bold black gaze steadily holding to Rita Drummond where she stood on across the rack from him. He looked to Sloan Verrill like a hot-blooded, reckless man; a bad one to cross.

Suddenly young Trent stopped talking and inched over to also peer ahead through the barn doorway. After a moment of bitter glowering he said softly, "I still think it was Mister Leonard got off with our cows."

Verrill looked down. "What cows?"

"We had thirty head. We were buildin' up to a decent herd by keepin' heifers and peddlin' steers. Last year I rode old Bally all over the country an' found only nine cows. This spring a few weeks back I rode all over, and didn't even find those nine."

Verrill put a thoughtful gaze upwards and outwards

35

where Rita Drummond and Shelton Leonard stood in bright sunlight. He thought that whether Trent was right in accusing Leonard or not, this was not a new story. Many a widowed ranch-woman saw her herd steadily dwindle until she ended up with nothing at all.

"Tell me about him," Verrill said. "How many head does he run?"

"Well; over a thousand cows an' bulls, I can tell you that," replied the lad. "I've seen him an' his men gather that many at one markin' time. But it's probably a lot more'n a thousand."

"How many men does he keep?"

"Three, besides himself. Two part-Indians and a real mean Mexican named Juan."

"He looks like a 'breed, himself."

"He is. My paw said he was anyway."

Sloan dropped his gaze again. This was the first time the boy had ever mentioned his father. Even when they'd stood up there by that side-hill grave, Trent had not spoken of his father.

Trent said, "His home-place is eight miles west of here, but he owns about thirty thousand acres, and his east boundary line is also our west line."

"Got a family?" asked Verrill.

Trent shook his head. "He was married once. I heard the riders talkin' about that one time up in the Basin at the supper-fire when they brought a herd up in the spring. They said his wife disappeared. I guess they meant she left him. When I asked 'em what they meant, they just started talkin' about something else."

Leonard straightened up off the hitchrack. This movement caught Verrill's attention. He watched the dark cowman move easily around the rack closer to Rita Drummond. He was talking and smiling as he did this, still with his hat far back so that sunlight struck down across his dark face. Rita retreated a step and half turned away towards the house. Leonard also turned. He became suddenly very still. He was gazing out through the trees and for a moment it did not dawn upon either Verrill or Trent Drummond what had caught Leonard's attention. Then Trent whispered fiercely: "Your bay horse. He's seen your bay horse."

This proved correct. Leonard was suddenly no longer interested in Rita Drummond. He was standing arrow-straight and unmoving, gazing straight up through cottonwood shadows where Verrill's horse stood drowsily hip-shot under a big tree, swishing his tail at flies.

Leonard swung his head, said something to Rita to which she did not reply, and started strolling over towards the pasture fence. He stopped, leaned upon an old fence post and studied Verrill's horse for a long time before turning and running a slow, alert gaze all around the empty yard.

Rita walked over and said something to Leonard which brought back his bold smile again. He lifted his shoulders, let them fall and straightened up off the post. This time, when he spoke, Verrill heard him.

"Wouldn't mind that at all," he said. "I was sort of

lookin' forward to sittin' in the kitchen with you today an' drinkin' some woman-cooked coffee for a change."

Trent sighed and said, "That was close, Sloan. If Maw hadn't asked him in for a cup of java he'd have walked up to the gate an' seen your saddle hangin' from the tree-limb sure enough."

Sloan said nothing. He too understood why Rita Drummond had done that, but this wasn't what was holding him there in the doorway. Sloan Verrill knew men; he'd known a lot of them who'd acted at one time or another exactly as Shelton Leonard was acting now. He watched Rita lead Leonard over to the back door, enter ahead of the lanky cowman, and he also watched the grinning, bold way Shelton Leonard also entered that house.

Trent said, "Come on, Sloan; let's finish the harness."

Sloan stepped over and began dipping and draining straps of leather again, but he kept watching the back of the house. There were a lot of Shelton Leonards in this world. Even in as remote a place as this, all it took to turn an otherwise normal man into one of them was the heady and voluptuous beauty of a widow-woman like Rita Drummond—and maybe a shot or two of strong whisky, or a little Indian blood.

They finished the second set of harness, set pans to catch the dripping residue-oil, cleaned up and carefully stoppered their oil bottles. From behind the barn Trent's milk cow lowed, and the boy went down through the building to open the back door for her. He turned as the cow walked in and said, "Hey, Sloan; how do you figure 'em? This morning she was wild-actin' an' this afternoon she's real tame and willing."

Sloan was drying his hands upon an old shoeing apron. He smiled as he watched the old cow head for her stanchion, poke her head through and begin eating meadow-hay from her manger.

"Just a woman," he said to the lad. "Just a female, Trent. There's no predicting them." He hung the shoeing apron back on its nail, let the boy walk up, then said, "That's why you don't see horsemen ridin' mares. One day they're as even-tempered as a man could ask, the next day they bog their heads when a bird flies out of a bush, and set a man afoot twenty miles from water."

Trent thought on this a moment and nodded. "I've heard that said before," he murmured. Sloan looked at the boy thinking that he could guess where Trent had heard it before, and also wondering, again, why Trent Drummond did not like to talk about his father. Then the boy's mind jumped to something totally foreign, after the fashion of boys and he said, "Sloan; we sure got a lot done around here since you rode in. Caught the cow, fixed the dam an' put the harness back in shape."

Sloan could see the forming idea in Trent's eyes before the boy formed it into words, and tried to head it off. But Trent was too quick for him.

"Why don't you stay on for a few days, Sloan? We

39

could have a lot of fun."

"Fun?"

"Well; there's some fence that needs mendin', and we could go swim up at the dam, an' maybe we could even go out and set snares for the wild horses."

Sloan eased down upon an up-ended horseshoe keg, pushed back his hat and relaxed. It was cool in the barn, and pleasantly fragrant from the loose hay stacked there. He sucked back a big breath and slowly let it out.

"You figure mending fence and trapping mustangs is fun?" he idly asked, his thoughts drifting on over to that cool kitchen inside the house.

"It would be fun if we could do it together," Trent said, and there was a sudden wistfulness in his voice which was not lost to the man. "Maybe Maw'd come along with a picnic-lunch like she did today. That'd make it fun, wouldn't it, Sloan?"

The silence beyond the barn was endlessly deep and all-pervading. Sloan considered his hands for a moment before he softly said, "Yes. I think it'd be fun, Trent."

"Then you'll stay on?"

Sloan lifted his smoke-grey eyes, looked at the boy's eager face, and shook his head. "It wouldn't look right," he said.

"What wouldn't look right?"

"Well. . . . Nothing, Trent. Anyway; I've got to be moving along. There's a heap of country between here and California. I'd sort of figured to be across most of it before full summertime comes. Doggoned uncomfortable ridin' over deserts in the summertime."

The boy's hopeful expression crumpled. To the watching man it seemed that disillusionment came too easily to Trent Drummond; it was as though he hadn't really expected a dream to materialise anyway; as though he'd learnt the bitterness of personal defeat long before and had come to accept it as a way of life.

"But maybe I could come back," he said quietly, reaching for something which would ameliorate the boy's crestfallen apathy. "Maybe next spring. Then we could do those things."

"Sure," whispered Trent, neither believing Verrill would ever return nor making any real attempt to sound as though he believed it. "Sure, Sloan."

"Well; let's milk that cow, then I expect I'd better catch my horse."

Trent looked long at the man as Sloan stood up, then turned quickly away walking blindly over where the milk bucket hung upon a nail. The man was too intently watching to catch the sharp, high cry from the house until it was repeated. Then he whirled around.

"That was Maw," said Trent, also abruptly electrified by that muffled scream, but burly Sloan Verrill was already out of the barn heading houseward in a run.

The third scream was more shrill, more full of writhing dread and terror. It rose quiveringly into the afternoon hush just as Sloan Verrill reached the back door of the house.

FIVE

SLOAN jumped through into the kitchen where a vivid scene struck him. Rita Drummond, her hair tumbling loose to her shoulders, was writhing in the powerful arms of swarthy Shelton Leonard, whose hatchet-face was oily with sweat and shades darker than normal from an infusion of hot blood. Sloan's sudden appearance caught Leonard entirely unprepared. He did not immediately release Rita, but his black eyes swung over, saw Sloan and steadily widened with purest astonishment. Even Leonard's expression changed. He suddenly dropped both arms. Rita staggered, put forth a hand to steady herself upon the kitchen table, twisted to follow out the wide-eyed stare of Leonard, and also saw Sloan Verrill standing there, his grey gaze on Leonard with a fire-pointed controlled anger.

Leonard was breathing hard. He said, "Who the hell are you?" to Verrill, and slightly hooked his right arm at the elbow until his fingers were only inches above a curling six-gun butt.

Sloan's lips lay flat against his teeth in a sucked-back way. "Don't touch that gun," he said. "Now pick up your hat, 'breed, and clear out of here."

That word ' 'breed' brought to Leonard's face a wild and unreasoning expression. He called Sloan a fighting name, and said, "She lied about that bay horse, didn't she? It wasn't no stray, was it?"

42

"It wasn't a stray, no," retorted Sloan. "And if you hadn't had somethin' else in mind you wouldn't have believed that. But your kind generally is stupid anyway; too stupid to live long except in an isolated country like this. Now pick up that hat and walk on out of here—while you still can."

Leonard's astonishment was atrophying. He was beginning to view Sloan Verrill in a different light now. His black eyes got sardonic, his coarse mouth drew slightly upwards. "You got the look to you of a feller who come down out of the north, mister. Like a feller who rid in here off the Tumbleweed Trail."

"And you," said Sloan, "got a belly full of words instead of guts—'breed."

Leonard's black eyes blazed. He closed his mouth and stood over there across the room making a careful assessment of Sloan Verrill. Off on his right Rita Drummond stood along the wall as still as stone, seeming scarcely to breathe. Behind Sloan in the doorway young Trent Drummond was also motion-less, watching and waiting, his violet eyes shades darker, his boyish expression showing that he was having trouble understanding all this.

"All right," said Sloan quietly to Leonard. "You look mad enough to try it. Go ahead—and I'll put three slugs through your guts before you clear leather."

"Gunman," breathed Shelton Leonard, completing his study of Verrill. "Gunfighter, ain't you?"

"Draw and find out."

43

"Rider off the Tumbleweed Trail—outlaw, ain't you, stranger?"

"You talk too much, Leonard. You got the kind of guts most 'breeds got; tackle a woman you figure is alone, then tuck tail when a man shows up."

Leonard was not going to draw; that became increasingly clear as the seconds slipped past. But he was not a coward and Sloan saw this too. He finally inclined his head and made a cruel smile.

"Out in the yard, gunfighter," he said. "Man to man. You want to settle up for this so bad, let's try it that way."

Sloan put his head slightly to one side. Shelton Leonard was a rawboned, sinewy man. He could kill with his hands, and for the repeated insults he'd taken in this kitchen, he would now try to kill. Sloan said, "Take off that gun-belt, 'breed, and walk on out of here."

Leonard bent slightly to obey. Sloan watched him intently until the taller man held forth his shell-belt, smiled and dropped the thing upon the floor.

Sloan jerked his head and stepped backwards for Leonard to pass on out of the house ahead of him. Young Trent backed away as Shelton Leonard moved doorward. Sloan was turning to follow along when Rita said softly across the room to him, "No; please don't, Mister Verrill. He has a reputation for fighting with his hands. He carries a knife. Please; just make him go away."

Sloan looked briefly at Rita's white, stricken expres-

44

sion, turned without speaking and hiked on out into bright afternoon sunlight.

Leonard had removed his sheepskin coat, had loosened his trouser-belt, and was standing wide-legged out there wearing that mirthless, cold smile of his. "The gun," he said to Sloan, nodding downwards.

Sloan loosened his tie-down, unbuckled his belt and slung the thing over so that it landed at Trent Drummond's feet. "Sort of keep an eye on it," he said to the lad. "And keep out of the way."

Leonard flexed his arms, opened and closed big bony fists, and lost some of his smile as he went into a crouch. "Soften you up a little, stranger," he growled over at Sloan. "Soften you up for the killin'."

"With your hideout knife, 'breed?" asked Sloan in a taunting tone. "You're the type to have a hideout knife."

Leonard narrowed his eyes, dropped his head down behind one curving shoulder, and moved in. He was no novice at this, Sloan saw at once, as he began balancing forward for their initial clash, but then neither was he a novice at what cowboys called "dog-fighting."

Rita Drummond came as far as the back door and stood there, one hand to her throat, the other lightly lying upon the door jamb.

Swarthy Shelton Leonard jumped in, swung, and jumped back. He missed with that one, circled, and tried the same manoeuvre again. As he sucked back from those blows Sloan Verrill began to form an idea about his adversary's tactics. Leonard had long arms; he would probably try for those long, reaching strikes in order to achieve his initial successes. Verrill stepped forward to feint Leonard into throwing another of those overhand, looping strikes, and when Leonard did exactly this, Verrill dropped low, lunged in under the thrown fist and ripped two blasting strikes wrist-deep into Leonard's middle.

Leonard's mouth twisted as he reached for air. Verrill had hurt him. He back-pedalled, trading space for time, managed to stay clear of Verrill until he got his wind back, then he sidestepped, forced Verrill off balance, and as Sloan twisted in the new direction, Leonard ran at him.

Leonard hit Verrill three times, hard and fast. These were stinging rather than hurting blows, but they demonstrated Leonard's incredible speed. Blood appeared at the edge of Verrill's mouth where knuckles had skidded over unprotected flesh. Verrill stepped back, expectorated and stepped in again.

Leonard circled, he weaved in and out. He softly called Verrill a name, and he flung sweat off his face with a sidewards fling of his head. He then stopped moving, settled down flat-footed, and when Sloan Verrill stalked him, Leonard catapulted himself forward. Verrill had time for a blasting uppercut, which missed, then Leonard was upon him with clawing hands and straining breath. Verrill was borne backwards by Leonard's momentum. The pair of them, locked in a fierce embrace, crashed into the house.

Leonard tried to bring up a knee to Verrill's groin. This was blocked by a twisted hip. He tried to hurl Verrill back, tried to slam Verrill's head against the rough logs. Verrill dropped low under those frantic claw-like hands, shot a short, solid strike into the 'breed's middle, shot another one blasting upwards to strike along Leonard's sweat-oily jaw and upwards, along the taller man's face. He then swung sideways as Leonard abandoned his grasping tactic and began also throwing punches. Verrill took most of these along the side from hip to shoulder. They hurt but did not daze him.

Shelton Leonard, in his savage wrath, then made a fatal mistake. He stepped back one foot to cock and fire his right. Sloan, with his own right already up and ready, put all his turning, twisting weight behind that upraised arm and beat Leonard to the punch. He was jarred by the solid, crunching impact of that strike. Leonard, leaning forward, took that fist over the heart. It knocked him backwards. He staggered, dropped both arms, twisted his face into a breath-gone expression and looked straight ahead out of glazing eyes.

Verrill went ahead, set one boot against the log wall for impetus, and lunged. He struck Leonard head-on. When the 'breed would have gone down from that collision, Verrill caught his shirt-front with one hand, struck him across the mouth, across the bridge of his hawkish nose, twisted with Leonard's sagging weight carrying him almost off-balance, and hurled Leonard up against the house.

47

The force of that striking big body made windows rattle. Over where Rita Drummond stood, came a gasp. Young Trent, his face white to the hairline, was biting his lip.

Shelton Leonard did not go down right away, Claret dripped from his smashed mouth, his eyes turned aimlessly in his head, but instinct and the log wall at his back kept him upright. Both his arms were down; he was helpless and beaten, only scarcely conscious, but still upright.

Verrill stood wide-legged sucking in great amounts of hot afternoon, sage-scented air. Then he stepped in, caught Leonard's belt, set his legs and strained back and around hurling Leonard twenty feet out into the yard. Now Leonard went down. Dust flew upwards where he landed. For a moment there was not a sound in the yard. The sunlight was reddening as afternoon advanced down across the land. The world was hushed and still until Sloan slowly turned towards Trent, held out his hand, and when the lad passed over his gunbelt, he clumsily buckled it around his waist with swollen hands. Afterwards, he straightened up saying, "Son, fetch us a bucket of water." His voice was as calm as it would have normally been.

Trent walked off like a person in a trance. He kept gazing at the battered, still form of Shelton Leonard all the way along.

Rita said softly, "Mister Verrill; come over into the shade. Your face is as red as a beet."

Sloan turned, considered the beautiful widow, then

faced back again. He did not heed her suggestion and he did not say a word back to her.

When Trent returned Sloan took the bucket, stepped over, toed Leonard over on to his back and unceremoniously dumped the entire contents of that bucket upon the unconscious man. Leonard made a weak, bubbly cough, rolled over, got both arms under him and pushed. He hung there on all fours dumbly shaking his head.

Verrill set aside the bucket, examined his badly lacerated hands, worked the right one open and closed to allay stiffness, and gradually got his breath back. By the time Leonard was able to draw up his knees and unsteadily stand erect, Verrill had retrieved his hat and had tucked in his shirt-tail. Not until then did he move back into the shade where Trent and Rita Drummond stood, by the back door.

The three of them watched Shelton Leonard until the cowman lifted his head, put up a hand to gingerly explore his broken mouth, and mumble thickly at Sloan Verrill.

"I'll kill you for this, stranger. If it's the last thing I ever do—I'll kill you for this."

Verrill said stonily, "Next time be plumb sober, Leonard, and don't try it alone. You're not man enough. Now get on your horse and get out of here."

Leonard's smoky gaze went past, caught upon Rita Drummond in her doorway and lingered there. "You dirty. . . ."

"Watch that!" snarled Verrill, stepping swiftly back

out into the punishing sunlight, his meaning starkly clear.

"You too," said Leonard thickly to Rita. "You too, by gawd. I'll settle with you too, for settin' me up for this."

Verrill moved ahead, caught Leonard by the arm, turned him and gave him a powerful forward shove. Leonard staggered but did not fall, in the direction of his tied horse.

Young Trent ran up to hand Verrill the beaten cowman's gun-belt, hat and sheepskin coat. Sloan took these things over, carelessly tied them to Leonard's saddle then gave the unsteady rancher a rough boost into the saddle. As Leonard bent to gather his reins Verrill put his face up close and said in a voice too low for Rita or Trent to hear, "Next time pick on a woman of your own kind, 'breed. If I ever see you around here again I'll kill you on sight."

Sloan stepped back, reached around and gave Leonard's animal a sharp slap over the rump. The horse jumped, startled by that unexpected strike, and lit out in a long lope.

For as long as it was possible to see Shelton Leonard, Sloan Verrill stood out by the hitchrack gazing after him. When the vanquished cowman topped out over the westward ridge and dropped abruptly from sight, Sloan turned to gaze back where Rita was standing with her arm around young Trent's shoulders. He neither walked over to those two nor spoke to them. He was thinking of Leonard's threat;

not his threat against Sloan, but his threat against the beautiful widow.

What deeply troubled him about this was simply that, as soon as he rode on his way, Rita Drummond would be entirely alone again and at the mercy of a man whom Sloan Verrill knew just well enough to realise that what he'd threatened to do, he would also concentrate upon actually doing.

He pushed up off the rack and slowly paced on over into the shade facing Rita and her boy. "I didn't help you any," he said. "I should've just run him off."

She shook her head. "You couldn't have run Shelton Leonard off any way other than the way you did, Mister Verrill. I know."

SIX

HE went alone out into the little fenced-in pasture where his horse stood, plucked a blade of grass and sank down there in pleasant shade to idly chew and think. It didn't occur to him that for the first time this day Trent Drummond was not dogging his heels until, some time later when the sun was beginning to sink lower down the westward sky, Rita came quietly walking out where he was.

She stood before him in a full-bodied, solemn way considering his swollen hands and the side of his mouth where Shelton Leonard's fists had scored, which was also swollen, and she said, "I thought it might be better if Trent didn't bother you for a while."

He gazed upwards. She was a wise woman as well as a handsome one. He did not think that wisdom ordinarily came to women at her age, and yet there was something in the depths of her eyes which said she'd lived a lot. Had come to know many things that ordinary women never knew at all.

He removed the blade of grass, tossed it away and said, "He was an outlaw, wasn't he?"

She didn't ask the obvious question. She simply sank down there in the grass near him and nodded. "Yes; he was an outlaw. I met him when I was fifteen. He was wild and handsome and laughed in a way that made my whole world light up. We were married." She looked at the hands in her lap. "One day he left me saying he'd go for two horses for us to ride away on. When he came back he had the horses. That night we left. We got as far south as Carson City by riding fast. Then he skirted around the town and made a camp in the foothills. That's where he collapsed and I found that beneath his coat he had a bullet-hole through the chest. While I nursed him there in our little camp he talked of many things while he was unconscious. And I found nine thousand dollars in his saddlebags from a Denver bank."

She looked up and around, her eyes grave and quiet. She lifted one hand to sweep back a tumbled-low heavy curl of coppery hair.

"I moved him when he was well enough to sit a saddle. I kept moving him every week or so. Once a posse almost caught us but I hid him in a cave and they swept past in the dusk. Later, I got him down here."

"He recovered, ma'am?"

"Well; he seemed to be better. The bullet had passed straight through. There was no infection but he coughed a lot and he tired easily. Still, we were safe here in this place, and we went down to Bidwell several times, no one knew him there. We brought back things for our buildings like hardware and nails, tin for the roofs. Things like that. He worked a little each day; it took a long time even with me helping him, but we did it. We built this ranch out of nothing, dammed the creek, completed the homesteading, finished our buildings. But he got a little more tired as the years passed. Some days he couldn't do anything but sit in the sun. We knew what was going to happen, and it did happen. Two years ago he died."

"Well," murmured Verrill softly, "maybe a doctor. . . ."

"No. A doctor would have asked questions. People with bullet-holes in them, particularly strangers, arouse curiosity. He said he'd rather die up here in peace then get patched up and spend the next ten years in prison."

"Yeah."

She swung towards him with dusk's soft shadows lying across her face. "Mister Verrill; you are a man who wonders about things. I've seen the questions in your eyes."

"It's none of my business, ma'am."

"Is it the boy?"

"Yes'm."

"He was dying, Mister Verrill, and dying men feel a terrible urgency. He never had time for the boy. He wasn't cruel to him, he just didn't have the time."

"I reckon," murmured Verrill, plucking another blade of grass. "Anyway, I'm not judgin' him. I didn't even know the man. It just struck me the boy's like an orphaned pup; he looks at you with a kind of pleading expression."

"It gets inside you, doesn't it, Mister Verrill?"

"It does, ma'am."

She drew up her knees, clasped her arms around them and sat regarding him with that steady, considering, smoky gaze of hers. "He wants you to stay very much. Mister Verrill, did you ever see anyone cry and not make a sound?"

He flung away the stalk of grass and lifted his head to face her. "You sure don't make it very easy to pull stakes, ma'am."

"Must you?"

"That's what I came out here to wrestle over. Leonard'll be back, Miz' Drummond. I know his kind. Maybe you know them too. He didn't hate you at first, but now he does. Now he wants to see you down on your knees, and he'll scheme ways to get you like that. There are men in this world who can hate with their whole heart and soul. Leonard's one of 'em."

"Mister Verrill?"

"Yes."

"You don't have to feel responsible. If you hadn't been here it would have been the same."

"Not quite," he said very dryly, dropping his eyes. "But now that's not the point."

"I have guns in the house."

He looked up wryly. "Yeah. They were in the house today an' you never got a chance to use them." He gravely shook his head at her. "You won't get a chance to use them next time either."

"But I don't want you to feel obliged to remain if you don't want to."

Verrill caught a furtive movement over by the gate and watched that area from beneath his hatbrim without seeming to. He spotted a head of tumbled, coppery hair through the fence in among a clump of bitterbrush, heaved a sigh and said, "Ma'am; that's just the trouble. I'm not so sure I don't want to stay."

She smiled at him, her violet gaze warm and candid. "Trent's world would be complete if you did."

"And how about you; folks got a bad habit of talking."

"Twice a year the cattlemen pass through here on their way into Bitterbrush Basin. They usually stop by to see how we are; to offer to fetch us in supplies when they send their wagons down to Bidwell." Rita Drummond shrugged. "Whatever talking they'd do, Mister Verrill, neither you nor I would ever hear."

"I wasn't thinkin' of you or me, ma'am. I was thinkin' of the boy. Some day he's goin' to have to go to some town for proper schooling and kids are cruel.

Right now you're the only person on earth he sets store by. Cruel kids and gossip could damage his image of you, and I'm wonderin' if you have any idea what it does to a man to have something he strongly believes in, turn into something he can't respect."

She kept watching his face. Even when he finished speaking she kept watching it. Finally she said quietly, "Would it make you feel any better to tell me about her, Mister Verrill?"

He straightened up off the ground, looked on over into that bitterbrush patch with his expression cold to the beautiful widow, and raised his voice to say, "Trent; no real man listens when other folks are talkin'. You go on back to the house or come on over where we are, but don't be skulkin' around like a cussed Piute."

Rita turned, surprised, and saw her son slowly rise up out of the yonder brush clump. She spoke his name in swift anger and would have said more but Sloan Verrill said quietly, "Stay out of this. I caught him at it. It's between him an' me."

She swung around, her violet eyes turning stormy towards the man, but he ignored her. "If your paw was here he'd tell you the same thing, boy. A man's above sneakin' up and listenin' like you've just done. Maybe you'd better head on back for the house and think about it a little. Go on, now. We'll be along directly. Then you can tell us what decisions you've come to."

Trent walked away with his head down and without making a sound. Sloan Verrill, watching, had a faint look of understanding amusement in his lingering gaze.

Rita said a trifle sharply, "I told you; he and his father had nothing in common. They hardly knew each other, Mister Verrill."

"Then it's time they did know one another," Sloan said, getting to his feet. "Let me tell you somethin' about boys, ma'am. Whether they knew their paws or not, they've got to believe in them. A step-father maybe actually does more for a boy, but in his heart the kid's got to have a solid picture of a great man for a paw. He doesn't know the outlaw part of it, does he?"

"No, of course not."

Sloan held down a hand. When Rita took it he lifted her to her feet and withdrew his hand. "You haven't been too wise a mother to him," he told her, "or you'd have tried to help him hold to that image of his dead paw. Ma'am; it doesn't matter how fine a mother a lad has, he's got to also have a fine paw—at least in his heart and mind he's got to have one."

She stood pale in the face with that dead-level gaze of hers unwaveringly upon Sloan Verrill. She whispered, "I never thought of that. I never knew. . . ."

"How could you know, ma'am. You're a woman." Sloan swung his eyes away, took in the barn, saw his outfit hanging near the pasture gate from the tree-limb, and said, "I never had trouble makin' decisions before. It's getting along towards evening. I'll bed down in the hay for tonight."

She put out a hand, lightly lay her fingers upon his arm and said, very, very quietly, "There's a spare room in the house, Mister Verrill."

He acted as though he hadn't heard that, moved out from under her touch and started forward. She halted him, brought him back around in the forming shadows of late dusk.

"Mister Verrill."

"Yes'm?"

"He'll be waiting over on the porch, and supper'll be ready in a little while."

He balanced there watching her for a long moment. She was softly lovely in the dying day. She was the kind of vision rangebred men carried in their hearts and minds. Those backgrounding big trees with their silver-green leaves and pale trunks, that underfoot thick matting of good green grass, the red shafts of filtered sunlight, all made a suitable setting for her beauty and her stillness.

He turned and walked on down to the gate, passed through it and turned, not towards the barn, but towards the house. He didn't look back at all, and when he found young Trent the boy wasn't on the porch, he was sitting on an edge of the well-box forlornly kicking one foot back and forth. He heard the ring of Sloan's spurs but he didn't look up.

Sloan halted, said gruffly, "Move over," and sat down next to the lad. He looked up at the murky sky and said, "A man sometimes does his best thinkin' at day's end." His voice was a soft drawl in the otherwise hushed world he and the lad shared. "Bright sunlight is a time for doing, but evenin' is a time for thinkin'. You agree?"

Trent nodded, still avoiding the man's face.

"You been thinkin'?"

"Yes."

"Want to tell me about it?"

"I'm sorry, Sloan. I shouldn't have done it."

Sloan put a thick arm over the boy's shoulders. "You know, son, there's just one thing worse in this world than makin' a mistake. That's refusing to admit you made one. Now let's forget it."

Trent raised his face to the man. "You said my paw would have said the same thing about me spyin' on you and my maw; do you believe that, Sloan?"

"Of course I believe it."

"But he hardly ever even talked to me, Sloan."

"He was a sick man, boy, and sick folks got bad troubles. He was a good man an' he loved you. That's what you want to remember about him."

"Well; he never went swimmin' up behind the dam with me, an' when he rode out he always went alone. He didn't seem to know I was alive, Sloan."

"Don't you ever believe that, Trent. He knew you were alive." Sloan removed his arm from the lad's shoulders, gestured around the darkening night with it. "Why do you reckon he worked so hard makin' this ranch? So you'd have a solid roof over your head, you an' your maw, an' a barn to put hay into, an' green fields for your animals. And, son, he knew his time was getting close so he had to work fast. He didn't have time for the little things, but he loved you and he loved your maw, an' he did everything possible to prove it. Just look around you. His love for you two is in every board on that house and on that barn out there."

Trent sat for a long while in solemn silence looking at the ranch buildings. He appeared to be really seeing them for the first time. Sloan watched him from the corner of his eye, waiting for him to speak. The boy never did speak, though, and even if he'd intended to he didn't get the chance, for his mother softly called to them both from over at the back door where she stood faintly outlined by a rising old yellow moon.

"Supper's ready, you two."

They got off the well-box and started along. Sloan said, "Tell you what; in the mornin' we'll saddle old Bally for you, I'll ride my own horse, and we'll go make a sashay out where those wild horses are. Seems to me what you need on this ranch is a few head of worthwhile young saddle animals. Tell me, Trent; do you know where those mustangs have their trails?"

The lad turned without speaking, lifted an arm and pointed northward to Bitterbrush Basin. His eyes were bright with a hot dampness and instead of saying a word, he gulped, sniffled, and ran on into the house.

Sloan stood outside a moment working the warp of his thoughts into some kind of a pattern. He washed at the basin and dried on the roller-towel, paused to cast a solemn look up at that old yellow moon, then he too passed on into the house.

SEVEN

O LD Bally was long in the tooth, hadn't won a single cup for perhaps eight years, and was grey above the eyes, but he was like many an old horse who had, in his prime, been the kind of animal men set great store by. As young Trent and Sloan Verrill made their way up through Tumbleweed Pass old Bally was alert and right up in the bit. Old or not, he was willing.

They halted on the downhill side of the Pass and the lad said, pointing off north-westward, "There's a spring about five miles off in that direction. It's the only clear-water spring anywhere in the Basin. That's where the mustangs get water and have their dusting places."

Sloan considered that immense treeless place and wagged his head. "We've got work ahead of us," he said. "Can't snare 'em because there are no trees, which means we'll have to build a waterhole-trap out of brush and wire. Well; let's go do a little explorin'."

They got to the waterhole before noon after making a big sashay out and around the empty countryside, which enabled Sloan to familiarise himself with the Basin. While they were eating, sitting cross-legged in the shade of their saddle animals, Trent gushed information about the Basin. Finally, he threw up his head northward and said, "I've seen 'em sweep down to this waterhole from up in that direction, as though

61

they maybe were up in the Moccasin Mountains."

"What'd they look like?"

The boy was candid. "Some were pretty scrubby, inbred horses, but there were some good ones among 'em."

"How many you reckon are hereabouts?" Sloan asked, making all this conversation the kind of talk which passed back and forth between two men, not a man and a boy.

"I don't know, rightly. But there's more'n one band. I've seen 'em lots of times. Maybe five, six bands, with thirty to sixty horses in each band."

Sloan chewed thoughtfully for a moment, raised his head and said, "Thirty head of broke saddle animals at, say, thirty dollars apiece—how much money you reckon that'd come to?"

Trent's forehead furrowed, his eyes dulled-out from inward concentration, he was grimly quiet for a long while, then he threw up his hands. "I don't know, Sloan. I'm not very good at ciphers."

Sloan went on thoughtfully chewing. When they'd finished eating and were getting back astride again, he said, "They got stores and schools and such like down at Bidwell, Trent?"

"Yeah. It's a regular settlement."

"Two days ride though, isn't it?"

Trent nodded, gathered his reins and went along beside his companion. "Takes two days with our team and wagon. Sometimes, on the way back loaded, it takes three days."

They headed on across Bitterbrush Basin. Once or twice Sloan commented upon the fuzzy little carpet of new grass they passed over. Another time he halted to study some barefoot horse tracks for a long while, and point out to Trent how these were obviously the sign of free-moving animals, probably wild ones.

"See there how that splay-footed critter hit deep down in the dirt there with his left front foot, then changed leads ten feet along and hit down hard with his right foot?"

"Yes."

"Well; if a man'd been sittin' atop that critter he'd have yanked him back an' made him stay in one lead or the other, so we can figure that horse didn't have a man on him."

They back-tracked this band, saw where they had indeed come straight southward down out of the Moccasin Mountains, then turned back. As they rode along with afternoon sunlight bringing on a soft haze, Sloan said, "We've got to find a place where we can drive with the team and wagon, get us a big load of faggots, then come on back to the waterhole and make our trap."

"Over on the property line westward there's a big brush patch, Sloan. We can drive to it real easy, then drive back up here through Tumbleweed Pass."

Sloan turned. "Tomorrow?" he asked.

Trent flashed a big smile. "Sooner we get started on the trap the sooner we get into the horse business. And without the cows any more, we're sure goin' to need something to make money with."

"Yeah," murmured Sloan, looking sombrely off towards the west, towards Shelton Leonard's range, "without those cattle we sure are."

They got back to the ranch an hour ahead of sundown. Rita was milking the cow when they rode in, got down and off-saddled. She came to the barn and listened with smiling eyes as Trent related everything they had seen over in Bitterbrush Basin. As the lad took their two horses away she put a soft gaze over at Sloan Verrill.

"I think a man gives a young boy a reason for living. Are you hungry—you two?"

Sloan thumbed back his hat, shook his head and made a slow smile over at her. "Not particularly," he said, "but startin' tomorrow he'll be hungry as a bear. We're goin' to take the wagon and start haulin' faggots to make a mustang trap over in the Basin."

She moved back into the barn, was gone a moment then emerged carrying the milk bucket. He stepped over, took the bucket from her and paced slowly along beside her. Trent came trotting up to them just short of the house. Sloan handed him the bucket. Without a word Trent went hurrying houseward with it.

"Ma'am," Sloan said, when they were alone in the soft-lighted yard, "I did some tall thinkin' today."

"Yes."

"Well; the boy can't add numbers worth a hang."

Rita Drummond's deep blue eyes got very still. She stood close to Sloan looking at him. She seemed suddenly apprehensive.

"Ma'am; spring's here and summer'll follow. There's no school in summertime. But next fall he ought to get some schooling."

"It's sixty miles to Bidwell, Mister Verrill."

Sloan rubbed his jaw, making a little scratchy sound. He looked ruefully at her. "He's thirteen now. He'll likely live to be seventy or more. That's an awful long time to spend regrettin' how ignorant he'll be unless he gets schoolin' now, ma'am. In the world of Trent Drummond learning's goin' to have a heap bigger place than it's had in the world of Sloan Verrill—and Rita Drummond."

"Mister Verrill. . . ." Rita turned towards the house, walked thirty feet along, then halted and twisted to gaze back at him.

Sloan said quietly, "I know. Sixty miles between you an' all you've got to show for thirty years of livin'."

Rita suddenly drew herself upright and came fully around towards him. She said in a wondering way, "You know, Mister Verrill, I don't believe I ever knew a man like you before. You're very understanding. In fact, you seem to know what I'm thinking almost before I do."

"Shucks, Miz' Drummond, it's not a matter of mind-reading at all. It's simply a matter of what's got to be done; what you've got to face up to."

She turned away, saying, "Supper's ready. Please— let's not talk any more about it. As you said—there's all summer ahead of us."

He followed her as far as the back porch. There, as she passed on into the house, he removed his hat, rolled under his shirt collar, and noisily washed at the outside wash-stand. Trent came out to do the same thing and afterwards they did what rangemen commonly do, stood around idly talking behind until they were summoned on inside for supper.

After nightfall came Sloan left the house, walked slowly towards his bedroll in the barn, and paused out by the pasture gate where soft, golden moonlight turned the distant mountains into great-hulking monoliths supporting a pale-lighted sky.

There was hardly a breath of air moving, and beneath the huge old cottonwoods lay corridors of darkness running spoke-like in all directions. It was the hushed and warm kind of night to bring on a man's most haunting memories, to bring him all the way down to melancholy, particularly if he stood out in it quite alone, as Sloan Verrill did. Or at least as he thought he did, until Rita Drummond spoke quietly from off on his right, down the old fence a short distance with her hair loosened to lie softly curling across her shoulders, with her lovely face lifted towards him with gentle moonlight lying upon it showing its flawlessness as well as its trust and its wonder.

"What is it in some men," she gently asked, "that makes them so totally different from other men?"

He half turned where he was leaning, watched her glide up closer, and said, "Maybe they aren't different at all. Maybe it's that other folks only think that they are. Men are pretty much the same. Some are better with words than others, better with horses and ropes."

"And guns. . . ?"

He swung back to gazing up the far sidehill through night shadows. "And better with guns."

"Do you want to tell me about her now, Sloan?"

He shook his head. "Talking doesn't help much." He faced half around towards her and leaned there studying her lips, her eyes, her wealth of coppery hair. "You're an understanding woman," he murmured. "How did you know?"

She put up her hands upon the top strand of wire looking slightly away from him. "Intuition. Women can feel things about men. Yesterday, when you changed the subject, I knew it was a woman."

"That's all?"

She swung her face to him, gently shaking her head. "No. Guns too."

"And how did you arrive at that?"

"When you challenged Shelton Leonard. He knew it too; he felt it the same as I did. You would have killed him. You were capable of doing it and also, you were fast enough with your gun to do it." She looked steadily up into his eyes. "Could I guess out loud how it was, with you?"

"I don't like this," he told her quietly. "I'm here, you're here and Trent's here. Out there on that sidehill is a grave. In it lies a man, and along with him lie some of a girl's best dreams of a life that never was.

With me it's the same. The past is over and done with."

"You haven't forgotten it, though."

"Nor have you, ma'am."

She looked out through the trees up that golden-lighted slope yonder, and she whispered, "One never forgets, of course, but there's something you don't know. Something I didn't know either, for a long time. A fifteen-year-old girl doesn't love. She knows wild and fanciful infatuation, not love. What can anyone know of love at fifteen?"

He didn't answer. He simply stood there watching her, seeing the lift and fall of her breasts, the steady way she looked up that far sidehill, and the way her heavy lips lay gently closed without pressure. She was in his sight very beautiful and very desirable.

"I thought all day about what you said of Trent's father. He wasn't what you've made him seem, Sloan. He didn't want a child."

"He's dead, ma'am, so he doesn't really matter any more. But the boy matters."

"Yes; that's the conclusion I reached just before you and Trent returned this evening, and of course you are right. The boy matters and the man is dead."

"You give a kid something worthwhile to hold to, ma'am, and it makes him a better man then he could possibly be, otherwise."

"I agree . . . Sloan?"

"Yes."

"Was she very lovely?"

He straightened up off the fence, his night-shadowed face turning stern towards her, his jaw taking on that tough-set stubbornness she'd noticed in him. He was, in her sight, a full man with all the force, the power, the quick, hard judgments of a full man. Several times now he had brusquely put her in a woman's place; once, when she'd started to reprimand Trent for secretly listening to them, and again when she'd touched this subject of that girl he'd known somewhere else, in another part of his life.

"She would be lovely, Sloan. You'd insist on that in a woman."

He said a little roughly, "It's too bad nature doesn't always put a good heart with a good face."

"Moonlight can be as blinding as summer sunlight, can't it?" she whispered to him. "I know, even though with me it was different."

He said nothing. For a long while the silence between them ran on before she spoke again, breaking it.

She said: "There was another man and you killed him."

He still stood darkly silent and still.

"Which is it that goes over all the trails with you, Sloan, her face or the dying man's face?"

"His. She wasn't worth it. She smiled when I told her. Did you ever see anyone smile that way? No. No, you wouldn't have, because as you said, we each have something to remember, but it's different. Maybe the only thing that's the same is the pain. I reckon pain's not much different, ever."

"So you rode down the dark trails, Sloan; running isn't the answer."

"What is; that's what I've been wondering ever since I saddled up and left. What is?"

She was slow answering, but ultimately she said, "Some day you'll find what the answer is." She drew back from the fence, turned and started back down towards the house.

He turned and watched her go, then he stepped swiftly after her calling softly ahead. "Rita."

She turned. He went down to her, leaned a little and kissed her upon the lips. Without a word he then turned and went on out to the barn.

EIGHT

FOR two days Trent and Sloan hauled faggots from the ranch up through Tumbleweed Pass and out into the Basin. They worked hard and came home tired each night. The third day they hauled wire from the ranch to the waterhole and began weaving their solid wall of stakes, setting cedar posts at six-foot intervals, and fastening their faggot-fencing to these posts.

The trap was round and had no gate at all, but Sloan made a length of smooth-wire fast to one gatepost, and when Trent watched with a wondering frown, Sloan wordlessly stretched that wire across the wide opening, brought forth the ground-canvas from his bedroll and tossed it over the wire so that the slightest breeze made the canvas quiver.

"You can't smell it," he explained to the boy, "but that old ground-cloth smells of camp-fires, man-sweat, and gun oil. There isn't a wild horse living who could be driven into that piece of canvas with a whip. He'd beat himself senseless against the back of our trap before he'd even go near that canvas. That's the gate."

Trent's eyes glowed with gradual understanding and admiration. "You've done this before, haven't you?" he said.

Sloan chuckled. "When I was your age. Later on, too, I trapped a few wild ones. Snaring them is easier, but you can't snare mustangs in country like this. Come on; we've still got to put up the wings."

"Wings?"

"You'll see," said Sloan, heading for the wagon.

The wings to their mustang trap widened outwards across the plain for nearly a mile like a funnel, the closed end of which was the trap itself, and the water-hole which their trap surrounded, was the constant inducement for the wild horses to brave this strange contraption with the man-scent to it.

As they finished making their wings Sloan leaned upon the southerly-most wing-post and gazed down that wide-mouthed funnel leading to the waterhole.

"As long as there's no other nearby watering place the horses will go in. It may take them a day or two to get up their nerve, but believe me, thirst is a powerful inducement."

"Where'll we be while they're making up their minds, Sloan?"

"Well; normally we'd be back at the ranch. In the first place it'll be a mighty long wait. In the second place, if we aren't around for them to smell or see, they'll overcome their fear a lot sooner. But, since you've never seen this done before, tell you what we'll do; we'll dig a couple of trenches man-length north of the trap, get down into them and cover ourselves with bitterbrush—then we'll lie absolutely still and wait." Sloan turned, his gaze speculative. "You have any idea how long we may have to lie out here without wigglin' an eyelash?"

"All day, maybe?"

"At least that long. That means no eatin', no drinkin' water, no moving at all, because a wild horse can spy movement a mile off, and he won't come near. Think you're up to it?"

"Did you do it like this when you were my age?"

"Yup. More than once."

"Well then I reckon I can do it too."

Sloan chuckled, they took the shovels and walked out to make their little shallow trenches, cut and pile their brush, and afterwards to each of them try the places for size and comfort.

"One time," Sloan said, as he stood up to beat dust off himself. "I was trappin' with Arapahoe Indians. We made pits and brushed 'em just like you an' I have done here. I got down into mine and was doin' just

72

fine. The wild horses came trottin' up where all of us could see them, an' I happened to glance down. There was a cussed scorpion as big as a man's hand crawlin' down into the trench. I didn't dare strike at him or holler, or even let on to the Indians he was in the hole with me. I lay there and must've sweat a gallon of water while the horses came pussy-footin' it up into the wings and on along towards the trap. All the time that dad-blasted scorpion kept crawlin' up towards me."

"Were you scared, Sloan?"

"Scared? Son, I was petrified. One good sting from that big devil an' I was a goner. I knew it. So did the Indians when some of them finally saw that critter crawl up on to my arm."

"What happened?"

"Nothin' much. The horses went into the trap, the feller with the wire gave it a tug, another Indian jumped and threw the canvas over the wire and we had the horses trapped."

"I mean—what happened with the scorpion?"

"Well; the old Indian I lived with ambled over with a little stick, put it down in front of Mister Scorpion, and when the critter climbed on to the stick the old man lifted him away, dropped him and beat him to pieces with the little stick."

"Gee. . . ."

Sloan cocked an eye at Trent. "You know why I told you about that?"

The boy gravely inclined his head. "If a scorpion

crawls in with me I won't move either," he said.

Sloan loaded their tools into the wagon, estimated the time of afternoon from a brief glance at the sun's position, then handed the lines to Trent with a careless homeward wave of his hand.

"Tomorrow morning we've got to be out here before sunup," he stated. "It'll be a long walk."

Trent looked quickly around, his voice showing amazement. "Walk. . . ?"

"Sure. We'll come down into the Basin on horse-back, but we'll have to hobble the horses a couple miles off and walk on over here. Tame horses spook mustangs almost as quickly as men do."

That's how they did it, the next morning. They left Verrill's big leggy bay horse with old Bally back by the Basin-side of Tumbleweed Pass, took three lariats with them, two sets of leather, Mormon hobbles, and struck out across Bitterbrush Basin on foot. And as Sloan had predicted, it was a long, tiring walk for both of them. But Trent at least had his boyish enthusiasm to keep him going. It was dark still, with just the barest showing of faintness over upon the eastern horizon when they finally got to those carefully brushed-over little shallow trenches which were side by side. Here, after fixing their gate wire so that he could yank it across the big opening when the time came for this to be done, Sloan got belly-down and put a finger to his lips. "From now on," he cautioned, "not a sound or a move. And remember, Trent, we may be here all day, so stick a pebble in your mouth and when you get thirsty or hungry, start wallowing the thing around."

The sun came up. It climbed steadily higher into the overhead sky bringing with it piled-up layers of shimmering heat. Trent lay as still as stone with just his eyes above the place where he lay hidden behind a shielding matt of bitterbrush. On his right twenty feet away, Sloan Verrill lay just as still.

The day wore along. At high noon with the sun beating straight down upon them, Sloan saw young Trent stiffen, his eyes drawn out into a long squint westward. He could safely have asked the boy what he'd seen, but Sloan remained silent. He'd made a particular point of being quiet and completely still. He couldn't very well break his own rule so he lay there rummaging the heat-hazed westerly distance seeking movement.

He saw it, finally; a scudding cloud of alkali dust rising up in the wake of a band of swift-running horses. The animals were coming on from the west now, but far back where the dust cloud still hung, it was easy to see that originally the mustangs had come southward from the distant Moccasin Mountains.

Sloan cast a final, anxious look over where the wire in his gloved hand was fastened upon the distant gatepost. He looked at Trent also, and found that the boy was as still as an Indian. Finally, Sloan put a straining look far ahead into the heat-shimmering west.

The wild horses came sweeping down upon their

waterhole all in a wild-rushing, bunched-up group. To Sloan it looked as though there were at least forty of them. They were well inside the wings of the trap before the outermost animals snorted and shied wildly where sunlight shone off tight-stretched wire. By then the leaders were less than a quarter mile out.

But now the horses caught that dreaded human scent. They slammed down to a stiff-legged, sliding halt. Some of them stood rolling their eyes and quaking. Others, not quite so upset, stretched their necks to sniff the onward air.

For the man and boy it was a tense moment. If the animals felt imminent peril they would wheel and dash out of there, and although they would eventually return, it might take another full two days before they did so.

The leader of this wild-eyed band was an old grey mare with a mane and tail chock-full of burrs until she looked almost weighted down by the load of matted hair she carried. She was scarred and gaunt-ribbed and totally useless as far as the man and boy were con-cerned, but she was wily. Her nostrils quivered as she tested the air. She flung her head around, squealed and fretfully pawed the ground. But she did not whirl and run, which was what obsessed the man and boy.

Finally, she took several tentative forward steps. When nothing untoward happened she took several more steps. When the other horses did not follow, but instead remained timidly back, some pawing, some softly nickering their uneasiness, the old mare threw up her head as though in disdain and loudly snorted.

Sloan had sweat running into his eyes making a salty sting. He dared not shake it off. On his left young Trent Drummond seemed scarcely to be breathing.

That old grey mare finally walked right up to the trap's opening, lowered her head, stretched her neck to its complete limit, and softly snorted as she peered inside, rolling dark eyes wildly from side to side. Behind her now, the other horses came edging along. They softly snorted as the wing-wires came in ever closer, funnelling them onward to the trap's entrance. They crowded up behind the grey mare pushing and nudging her. She resisted this rearward pressure for a while before taking one mincing step inward. Ahead of her no more than a hundred feet, was the waterhole. She appeared to be very thirsty; she kept softly distending both nostrils, making that very faint snorting sound, but she also kept moving towards the water.

Sloan was not able to see the grey mare. In fact, as each succeeding horse entered their solid-walled faggot corral, he was unable to see those other animals either. He was instead concentrating upon the last few animals. These beasts seemed agonisingly slow in their progress. They would of course enter now, because all the other horses were inside, but they did so with great apprehension and with every muscle keyed to explode at the slightest untoward sound or movement.

Then the last animal stepped in. Sloan raised up, flung away sweat and yanked their wire. He jumped over, handed the wire's loose-end to young Trent, said, "Hold on tight. Don't let it sag," then sprang back, scooped up his bedroll-canvas and raced up to fling it over the gate-wire.

Not until he did that did any of the horses see him. In fact, the only direction available to them to sight in, was out over that canvas-covered wire, westward. Every other direction was entirely blocked off by the eight-foot-high faggot fencing, and although even the weakest animal among them could have easily broken through that fencing, as long as none of them could see through it they assumed that it was indestructible and did not try.

Sloan stood beyond the canvas gate. He beckoned for Trent to make his end of their gate-wire fast to a post and come ahead to inspect their catch.

The horses milled, reared over one another's backs and whistled in fright. But as long as that canvas hung there with its man-smell, not a one of them would attempt breaking past it.

Trent came gliding up, eyes alight with excitement, with triumph, lips parted, and his face red-flushed from the interminable, long wait under that fierce sun.

"Got 'em," he muttered inaudibly. "Got every one of 'em, Sloan?"

Verrill looked down and around. He too was smiling.

"Sloan; *we did it!*"

"Yeah, we did it. But this is only the beginning."

"What do we do next?"

"Well; we sit down here and sort of look 'em over. They need the time to quiet down—and I think you do too. Then we start figurin' which ones we'll rope and keep, and which ones we'll turn loose—like that scarred-up old grey mare—so she can go back and raise some more colts."

"Sloan; you goin' to *rope* 'em?" asked Trent, incredulously. "They're wilder'n deer."

"Not by the neck, boy. By the forefeet. We'll up-end them one at a time, put the Mormon hobbles on 'em, and maybe tomorrow we'll be able to get in there and get a squaw-bridle on 'em?"

"A squaw-bridle?"

"It's a rope halter mustangers use when they're breakin' the wild ones to lead, Trent. Remember, we've got to get these horses back to the ranch where there are decent corrals before we can start breaking them." Sloan shot a look at the sun. "Tell you what," he said. "You go back and fetch up our horses. All right?"

"Sure, Sloan. Anything you say. Gee; Maw won't believe this when I tell her we got forty head of wild horses."

Sloan smiled and watched Trent start trotting out across the trackless waste towards Tumbleweed Pass and their horses.

NINE

B Y the time they got home that particular night after trapping their wild horses the moon was up and Rita was worriedly awaiting them upon the porch. As they rode in and Trent rushed ahead to tell his mother of their success, Sloan saw Rita raise up, put something against the log wall and walk down to her son. He dismounted, looped his reins at the rack, stepped around Trent and his mother, stepped up on to the porch and stood there gazing at the log wall. A Winchester carbine was leaning there.

Rita came along with her arm around Trent's shoulders. She gazed at Sloan and made a small, forced smile. "Supper's probably cold by now," she said. He heard the coolness and understood how it was with her.

"I'll go round back and wash up," he said, moving off.

But he didn't do that, not right away. He cared for their horses, then he walked far up a sidehill quartering back and forth, found nothing and didn't really expect to find anything, walked back down to the barn, explored it thoroughly, then he went over and washed, combed his hair and went on into the kitchen.

Rita was putting food from the wood-stove oven upon the table and lifted her eyes to him as he came into the lamp-lighted room. "I was worried," she said softly. "You were gone all day."

Trent rushed outside to also wash. As he went through the doorway Sloan said, "I know. I guess I should've figured you'd worry about him. I'm sorry."

She relented towards him and smiled. "I imagined a hundred things had happened. You two got trampled by mustangs, or set afoot out there, or bitten by snakes."

"Quite an imagination," he said evenly, watching her face. "But I reckon you had reason to worry. Who was it?"

"What?"

"Who was it you saw today that made you get the carbine?"

She drew upright and leaned upon a chair-back across the table from him. "You're like an Indian," she murmured. "You don't miss a thing, do you?"

He went over and pulled out a chair, sank down and cocked his head at her. "You can answer when you're ready," he said quietly, and sat there waiting.

"Well; about noon I went out to the sidehill to see if I could make either of you out over by the Pass."

"And?"

"There was a horseman sitting upon the westward ridge."

"Recognise him?"

She shook her head. "No; but I had a bad feeling, so I came back here, got the gun, and sat outside waiting."

"And you figured, whoever he was, he might have waylaid us. Is that it?"

"Yes."

Trent came rushing back into the room, hurled himself into a chair and reached for the platter of meat. Sloan looked over at the boy with a little gathering frown. "Pardner," he said, "a feller usually waits until the womenfolk sit down, then he passes them the food first."

Trent wilted, sheepishly pushed the platter towards his mother, and when she had helped herself he looked up. Sloan grinned at him and nodded.

They ate, neither the woman nor the man saying much. Trent graphically explained each detail of their success to his mother. He surprised Sloan with the way he remembered even the least significant details of their day's adventures. When he eventually ran down and a little moment of quiet came, Sloan said, "Tell you what, Trent; tomorrow we'll load a few flakes of loose hay on to the wagon, you take it out to our herd and toss it into the trap, then come on back."

"I thought you said we'd go back and hobble the best ones tomorrow," Trent said, gazing steadily across the table.

"Well; I did say that. But maybe the horses need an extra day of settlin' down. It sure won't hurt 'em and it might help 'em. Now when you're out there, don't spook 'em. Just toss 'em the hay and come straight back. You understand?"

"Sure. Then day after tomorrow we'll go out and hobble the ones we figure to keep?"

"Yep."

Sloan finished eating, drank his second cup of coffee thoughtfully, and afterwards got up and walked on outside. He was forking hay on to the old wagon when Rita came out to him later, watched him work for a while and said nothing until he'd completed the loading, hung up the pitch-fork, walked on over to her and said, "That wasn't very subtle, was it, tellin' him to take hay out to the horses?"

She shrugged. "He saw nothing wrong with it. But what troubles me is that he'll be alone out there, Sloan."

"That doesn't trouble me. What I've been turnin' over in my mind is just how I'm goin' to explain puttin' a dummy stuffed with hay on the seat beside him."

She looked blank. "A dummy?"

"Whoever was watching the place today probably has also been watching it yesterday and maybe the day before. He knows by now that Trent and I ride over into Bitterbrush Basin every day. He may even know why we've been goin' over there. Tomorrow he'll be expectin' to see two of us drive out of here with the wagon load of hay."

"I see," she murmured.

"Then tell me how I'm going to explain about the dummy to him, ma'am."

She shook her head, saying, "Would that really be necessary? Maybe, if the wagon goes out before sunup, from the ridge up there that watcher will assume both of you are on it. He won't be able to see much more than the team and wagon from that distance, in that poor light."

Sloan smiled. "For a woman, ma'am, you've got a good head on your shoulders."

She looked wry. "For a man that must be a hard concession to make."

His teeth whitely shone in the star-washed night, but only briefly. He twisted to run a gaze up along the faraway ridge westward. "Probably Shelton Leonard," he said. "He'd be recovered by now."

"No, it wasn't Leonard. He's a tall man. This rider was shorter and broader."

Sloan swung back towards her. "You've had all day to imagine who he was; what did you come up with, ma'am?"

"Juan Cortez, Shelton Leonard's Mexican range boss. He's a shorter, heavier man, and he'd be capable of sitting up there in the hot sun without moving for two hours the way that man did, watching the ranch."

Sloan leaned upon the wagon remembering something Trent had said about this Mexican. He was mean, Trent had said. The way he'd said it had impressed Sloan at the time; there had been strong feeling in the boy's voice.

Rita, watching Verrill's shadowed face, murmured, "Would Shelton send him down here for revenge, or was he only supposed to make certain I was left alone each day?"

"There's just one way to get the answer to that, ma'am. Send the wagon out at dawn like you said.

That'll get Trent away from here too, which might be a good thing. I've known my share of those Mex rangeriders. When they're your friend they'd die for you."

"And when they aren't your friend?"

Sloan pushed upright, sidestepped answering that question and said instead, "Did you send Trent to bed?"

"Yes. He was worn out."

"Maybe we worked a little too hard today."

"No. No, I didn't mean it to sound like that. Sloan; I've never seen him as happy as he's been these past few days. He worships you."

"You were angry when we rode in tonight, ma'am," he said, reminding her of the coolness she'd shown towards him at the front porch.

"That was relief. I was so relieved when you two finally came in I didn't know whether to thank God, or. . . ." She shook her head at him making no attempt to finish the sentence. In a softer tone she said, gazing into his eyes, "I had no idea you were so sensitive."

"Where you're concerned I am," he retorted, and started to turn away. He hadn't meant to say that, and yet he'd been thinking it.

"Sloan?"

He paused and turned back.

"Goodnight."

He stood there looking back at her saying nothing. The night around them was still and fragrant, starshine lay over the roof of their world with a mellowness

which the land rarely had in broad daylight. It was for
Sloan Verrill a confused and confusing time. She
pulled him against his wishes with her compelling
sturdiness and her beauty. During each day she was
brisk and efficient, but in the evenings she shook out
her wealth of thick, coppery hair and seemed entirely
different. She was the kind of a woman who seemed
perfectly attuned to the ways of daytime and night-
time.

"Goodnight," he said, at length, and added: "Don't
let Trent over-sleep. I'll have the wagon ready come
dawn."

He walked on over to the barn wishing powerfully
that he might turn and go back out to her. He had
kissed her once, but in a different way from how his
mind was running now. Then, it had been a meeting of
their lips in poignant understanding and honest sym-
pathy. He put a hand upon the door jam gripping hard.
If he went back and kissed her now, it would be alto-
gether different.

He heard her softly moving along towards the house
and turned to watch her fade out in formless shadows.
She was a beautiful woman, but more than that, she
was mature and wise and understanding, which were
the values a man in his thirties hoped for in a woman.

Then she was gone, the night ran on, and Sloan went
ahead to his bedroll. He could not right away drop off
though, even though he was tired. There was a deep-
down restlessness which tormented him for a long
time. In fact, before he finally slept, the moon had

soared almost directly overhead flooding the land with its soft-sad brightness.

He awakened shortly before dawn by simply opening his eyes. He had that inherent ability possessed by most men who live close to nature, to awaken when he wished. He went over to the creek, washed in water so cold it cleared the last cobwebs from his mind, went back and caught the team. He had them harnessed when the lamp came on down at the house. It was a warm morning, which meant it would be a hot day, the air was unmoving and clear as a bell, which made that little square of light down there stand out in the otherwise gloom, diamond-clear.

Trent came out where he was finishing the hook-up, and boy-like he was clear-eyed and interested. He had a little bundle tied in a gingham napkin which he put upon the high seat, then he went to the barn and returned with a pitchfork which he stabbed hard down into the hay. By then Sloan was finished and they met near the nigh-wheel, the one Trent would use to climb upon to reach the overhead high seat.

"Wish you were comin' along," the lad said, searching Sloan's face for some indication this might be so.

"You don't need me, son," said the man. "Besides, there's things got to be done around here before we can bring our horses in."

"Well," said the boy, putting a hand upon the nigh-wheel preparatory to climbing upwards, "I reckon you're right. For one thing, that snubbin' post in the main corral, it's about rotted off at the ground." He heaved himself up over the wheel, balanced up there briefly before springing to the seat. "And some of the stringers are only wired together. I expect they got to be fixed too, if we figure to keep 'em in our corrals."

"Yeah," murmured the man. "There are things got to be done. And Trent; just drive out, toss them the hay and come right back."

"You'll need me?"

"Pardner, I couldn't begin to do all this by myself."

Trent seated himself, unlooped the lines from the brake handle, set his foot against the brake-release and evened-up the lines. "I'll get back as soon as I can, Sloan," he said, and manfully kicked the brake-release off, flicked his lines and tossed Sloan a nod. "See you this afternoon," he called downward, and tooled his load down past the house, out into the westward country, then eased around and headed arrow-straight for dark and dimly-visible Tumbleweed Pass.

Sloan stood there watching him go overland towards the Pass with a little grin down around his lips. At thirteen a boy alternated between being a man and a boy; sometimes the changes were so swift that, one moment, a lad talked and acted like a grown man, and in a twinkling he was not a man at all, but a little boy again.

Sloan alternated between watching the wagon and the murky sky. He thought Trent had started early enough but he did not feel easy until the wagon disappeared into Tumbleweed Pass with all the gloominess of that confining place dripping solidly down over the outfit making it impossible to make out whether there was one person up there on that high seat, or two people.

He felt certain that if he could not tell from this much closer distance, then anyone watching from farther out would be even less able to discern that Trent was alone.

He turned and looked up the westerly slope to its top-out. He could make out nothing up there, and in fact he didn't believe there was a watcher up there yet. What he thought was that, later on when the watcher appeared, he'd be able to see the dust and the wagon far out over Bitterbrush Basin, and because his vigil had shown him that where Sloan went young Trent was also along, he'd think both the man and the boy would be riding along across the wastelands on that wagon.

If the watcher was fooled, and Sloan could think of no reason now why he would not be fooled, today might very well prove to be the time for Shelton Leonard to make his attempt at vengeance.

From down by the house Rita Drummond appeared, calling softly out towards the barn. "Coffee's on, Sloan."

He started ahead towards the house thinking someone today was going to be mightily surprised, when they came loping into the Drummond-ranch yard.

TEN

THE morning wore along. Dawn came with its soft-blushing pinkness, and later on, when the sun appeared over some easterly jagged peaks, a hard yellow brightness evolved out of the softer shades. This yellow light remained, sometimes shimmering far out where a breeze ruffled it, and sometimes lying like golden coloured lead in the valleys and arroyos.

The heat piled up before noon, there was not a sound anywhere, little dust-devils hurried past a mile out without aim or direction, and dissipated themselves when their motivating little ground-swell winds atrophied.

Sloan made an excursion up to the log dam with his Winchester lying easy in the crook of one arm. There was nothing up there but invitingly clear, blue creek water. He made a sashay down around the horse pasture to make certain his bay horse would not inadvertently amble out where he could be sighted and perhaps shot by one of Leonard's men, and after that with nothing more to do but wait, he selected a good shady spot at the base of a giant old smooth-trunked cottonwood and eased down there in such a way that he could command a full roundabout view.

The bay horse came over to explore Sloan's hat, his ear, and finally, satisfied, to stand there with a full gut, drowsing. There did not seem a more peaceful place on earth than this little hidden fold in the dun-grey hills, and only one thing kept Sloan from drowsing too. Ahead of him up the northerly slope lying pitilessly exposed under the bright sun, was the grave of Rita Drummond's husband.

Sloan sat there solemnly considering that grave, thinking some odd thoughts about that dead man, and when the quick, bitter reflection of hot sunlight off metal up along the western ridge suddenly struck flashingly down the hill, Sloan saw it at once.

He did not move at all except to turn his head the slightest bit. But watch as he might, he never again saw the reflection, nor for that matter, the man who had been up there to make it.

The sidehill was covered with short scrub brush all the way down to that grave out there with its upright headboard. A man might, with a lot of luck and experience, crawl on his stomach the full distance, and in fact not too many years earlier marauding Piute warriors would have attempted exactly that. But this would not be a bronco Piute, Sloan felt; it might be a 'breed Indian or a burly Mexican, or perhaps even Shelton Leonard himself, but regardless of who that was up there along the ridge, he was not going to waste half a day crawling like a snake through thorny brush.

Sloan heard a little sound and swung around. Rita was there standing utterly still in shadows with her Winchester. He said quietly and gruffly, "That's a good way to get shot, ma'am."

She didn't answer for a long time. She was effectively camouflaged by tree-shade. She was staring from narrowed eyes up towards the west ridge.

"There is a man up there," she ultimately said, speaking so softly Sloan scarcely heard what she said.

"I know. I saw his rifle-barrel reflection a minute ago. Rita; go on back to the house and stay out of sight."

She didn't go and Sloan did not speak to her again for quite a while because there came down the still air a soft sound of shod hooves moving over stony soil. A rider appeared up there against the skyline, a short, burly man on a husky, short-backed bay horse. The rider had his carbine lying across his lap. He sat up there without moving for as long as it took him to make a very careful study of the quiet, seemingly unalarmed and empty green patch down below. Sloan could not make out the man's face beneath its broad hatbrim, but he could tell from the way that man was sitting up there, that no movement, no building, no shadow, failed to get that watcher's fullest scrutiny.

For a full half-hour the man sat up there without moving. "Just like he did yesterday," whispered Rita from her place of safety deep in among the old cottonwoods. "Sat up there staring down here without moving."

"Don't you move either," muttered Sloan. "Be quiet as a mouse. Tell me something; did he have his carbine over his lap like he's carryin' it now?"

"No."

Sloan grunted. The rider was moving, was reining off northward along the ridge. "Hold your breath," he said to Rita back there in the gloomy shade behind him. "I think he's decided to come down and pay you a call."

They watched the horseman pass along several hundred yards atop his ridge before finding a game-trail to suit him. He then switched direction and came down towards the open sidehill where the grave was.

Sloan made a private observation about this stranger. He was a Mexican, but more than that, he was also an experienced gunman. This fact was obvious from the way the man wore his weapon tied-down and tilted forward for swift access, but also in his flesh-out holster. Very few rangemen carried their six-guns in specially made holsters like this man did, and only professionals advertised by wearing holsters with the hair-side of the leather, which was the smooth side, turned in, while the flesh side of the leather, or the rough-side, was turned outwards. The approaching Mexican was a killer.

Sloan eased around, got to his feet, kept trees between the oncoming rider and himself, moved down where Rita stood pale in the face watching that dark, burly horseman, and softly said to her, "Go on back to the house, but don't enter. Stay outside in the yard where I can keep watch over you."

She looked up at him, over his shoulder up along the west ridge, then jerkily nodded her head and turned away. His last words to her were: "And put that Winchester out of sight. Even a gunfighter isn't goin' to shoot an unarmed woman, but an armed one could be something else again. Get rid of it."

She did. Just before she walked on out into the yonder yard she leaned her carbine against a cottonwood tree.

Sloan stepped over behind a tree, swung and watched the Mexican. He was less than a half mile off now and riding along towards the house with his head up, his dark eyes constantly moving back and forth, in and out among the buildings, among the trees, never still. He did not seem in the least troubled nor apprehensive, simply interested in his surroundings and careful.

When the Mexican first spotted Rita, Sloan saw him draw up straighter in the saddle. She was over by the clothes line. Sloan had to admit to himself that she looked very normal fussing there with the drying wash. She made it a point never to see the Mexican. Sloan grimly smiled at her acting as he looked out, saw how the Mexican was passing completely eastward of him, and began gliding down closer to the trees directly behind Rita Drummond.

The rider was all eyes for handsome Rita. He had already made his careful study of the roundabout terrain anyway, not just as he'd approached either, but for some days previously, so now he rode into the yard with a lack of stiffness and a wide, wolfish grin, and when Sloan heard him speak he immediately placed the Mexican as one of those cowboys who had not only been born and raised north of the international boundary, but who infrequently despite the incongruity of it, could not speak Spanish at all. These *norteamericano* Mexicans were no different than any other North American except that outwardly they were Mexicans. This was one of that rare breed; his English was without accent and his words were the same as any other unschooled rangeman as he drew rein, looked down at Rita and leaned there with both hands clasped over his saddlehorn.

"Well now, ma'am," the Mexican said, through that bold, tough smile of his, "nice of you to be out here waitin'."

Rita turned with her back to the closest cottonwoods and looked straight up into that unpleasant smile. She did not say a word.

"Been sort of waitin' to catch that boy-friend of yours alone, ma'am," exclaimed the Mexican, "but just don't seem to ever make the right connections."

As he finished saying this the cowboy leaned outward and swung down. He moved up to the head of his horse and stood there. He looked around the quiet yard, let his gaze linger longest on the house, then eventually turned back to facing Rita.

"That was a bad thing you tricked Mister Leonard into the other day, ma'am. He's pretty mad about that. You know, when Mister Leonard gets mad and makes threats—he don't fool around."

For the first time Rita spoke. She had one hand lying lightly upon a clothes line pole while she regarded that dark, cruel face opposite her. "That's why you're here, isn't it; to make good his threat?"

The Mexican gazed at Rita for a long time without answering. He made that same mirthless smile again. "Maybe. Maybe not. Yeah, he sent me over here, but whether I do what I'm supposed to, or not, depends on you."

"Does it?"

"Yes, ma'am." The Mexican abruptly turned, walked his horse to the hitchrack, made him fast there and started back towards Rita. He wasn't smiling now but his muddy-coloured eyes were unnaturally and hotly bright and large.

She did not cringe as that unkempt man with his obvious intentions came forward. She said in a voice showing only the slightest bit of strain, "What did Shelton Leonard tell you to do, or is that a secret?"

The Mexican stopped. "No secret," he answered, his voice sounding husky now and rasping as his gaze burned into her. "He told me to fix you so's no other man would ever look at you again." The Mexican bent, lifted one trouser-leg to show the walnut handle of a boot-knife, and curled his fingers around that handle. He was bent over like that when Sloan Verrill stepped sideways from around a tree thirty feet behind and to the right of Rita Drummond.

The Mexican seemed suddenly turned to stone. He saw Sloan over there but acted as though he couldn't trust his own eyes. All that cruel boldness died out across his face. Even his hot, fierce eyes turned different, turned suddenly astonished, then, a moment later, turned calculating. He started to straighten up without the boot-knife.

"No," said Sloan softly. "Stay as you are, mister. Because when you straighten up I'm goin' to have to kill you, which I don't want to do just yet."

The Mexican stopped moving. In his bent-over posture he could not possibly draw and fire, though, so he hung there coldly studying Verrill and willing for as long as it was necessary, to prolong this confrontation.

"Leonard sent you to kill her?" asked Sloan.

The cowboy shook his head. "No; only to ear-mark her a little and cut off the end of her nose."

Rita's eyes grew enormous as she listened to this barbaric statement, but Sloan Verrill's reaction was more sanguine. He said, "Not much of a man, is he, this Shelton Leonard; why didn't he come over and do those things himself?"

The Mexican shrugged and said nothing for a while. He finally muttered something about that bent-over posture paining his back, then he said, "Mister; you got the drop now. You'll never get it again. If you're smart you'll saddle up and ride on—far and fast— because from today on there'll be a bounty on your head at the Leonard ranch. If I don't collect it, and if Mister Leonard don't, there will be other fellers who will. You can't win against all of us."

"No?" said Sloan. "Up to now I'm managin' to hold my own, cowboy. First Leonard, now you."

"You tricked Leonard an' you tricked me. Either one

97

of us could have killed you in a fair fight."

Sloan smiled thinly. "I don't know what Leonard told you boys at the ranch, but I'll tell you what really happened here. I gave him a chance to go for his gun an' he wouldn't. He was afraid to. So we used fists an' I cleaned his plough."

The Mexican gently wagged his head back and forth. "That's your version," he said. "But it's not the truth."

"Straighten up," said Sloan suddenly, and did not move from the slightly knee-sprung little crouch he was in. "I've been wonderin' how I was going to justifiably do this. Now you took care of that for me, Mex. You just called me a liar."

The Mexican came up slowly. For the first time since riding into the yard he seemed to be having second thoughts. He considered Sloan Verrill carefully. It was obvious that Verrill did not fear him at all. It was also obvious that the Mexican was not the only one in that yard who wore his gun low-lashed and tilted forwards in the classical position of gunfighters.

The Mexican licked his lips. He had now completely forgotten that Rita Drummond was anywhere around. He said, "Stranger, I don't think you can do it."

Sloan watched the Mexican's eyes, saw uncertainty show in them. He said quietly, "I think I can, cowboy. In fact I'm so sure I'm bettin' my life on it."

The Mexican started to say something more. He parted his lips but Sloan's one, spat-out word, quivered across the hush between them and the Mexican never got his chance to speak.

"Draw!"

The Mexican's right hand streaked downward as his body bent inward, as his obsidian eyes in their muddy whites turned fierce and lethal. Opposite him Sloan Verrill seemed to scarcely move at all. His right hand was a blur which suddenly blossomed into a great orange flash.

The Mexican's gun was swinging free of leather when the slug struck him. He was fast, very fast, and perhaps that is why he took Verrill's bullet and stood over there looking dumbfounded.

He tried to lift his six-gun, couldn't, stood a moment staring out of glazing eyes, then he fell with a soft-rustling sound, dead as he struck the ground.

Rita had the back of one hand across her mouth. She was staring from a waxen face at the dead gunman. She didn't look away from him until Sloan woodenly walked over, picked up the dead man, slung him loosely over his saddle face-down, and lashed him there for the long, grisly trip home. Then, as Sloan turned the horse, pointed it westward and slapped it, Rita looked at Verrill's sun-layered, hard and willing profile.

ELEVEN

SLOAN said nothing to Rita. He in fact avoided her entirely as he went up into the pasture, caught his leggy bay horse, saddled it and rode up through the trees towards the westerly ridge. He wanted to be certain the animal bearing that dead gun-fighter kept heading straight for the Leonard place. He also wanted to look northward from that eminence for some sign of young Trent.

He saw both; saw the Mexican's horse ambling towards home with all the willingness of a wily animal who knew where the hay and water were in this world, and also, off against the dust-setting of Tumbleweed Pass, he sighted the wagon returning. At the rate young Trent was travelling it would be long into the afternoon before he drove into the yard, but Sloan knew strong relief merely at the sight of him.

He had a third reason for riding up to the skyline away from the ranch. No rational man liked to kill, and afterwards there was always that moment, some-times short, sometimes long, of solemn reflection. It was much better for a man to be by himself at that time.

He dismounted atop the westerly rim, sat with sun-light pushing hard against him, plucked a dry grass-stalk and idly chewed it as he watched the Mexican gunfighter's horse walk steadily back the way it had come, growing smaller as the miles passed under its progressing hooves.

He also watched young Trent moving ant-like along his southward route towards the ranch. Then he saw something which completely overshadowed all his more sombre reflections. Coming on northward under a large dust-banner looked like what had to be a large band of horsemen. Actually, all Sloan could make out with any degree of fidelity, was that big, rising-up cloud of dust. What he was sure would be a large party of riders were miles off and even in that dustless, crystal-like clear atmosphere, it was impossible for him to make out any details at that distance.

He got back astride, turned and rode down the slope back towards the yard, but he did not go near the buildings at all, he instead cut on southward up along another sidehill and made a second, long study from that closer eminence. But the distance was still too great.

He finally, with afternoon shadows creeping out along the east side of things, left off straining to identify that slow-riding, advancing bunch of horsemen, or what he took to be horsemen, and went on down to the ranch. He off-saddled near the pasture, turned out his horse, took his carbine and started across through the trees towards that nearest sidehill beyond the grave. He did not look back to see whether or not Rita was down there at the house; he thought she'd be inside where it was cool, and where she could be reflective. He didn't particularly wish to face her just yet anyway. He felt no actual guilt about killing Shelton Leonard's Mexican gunfighting foreman, but he still had that little wish to be alone. It would remain with him a while yet.

He walked almost to the rim of the northward slope meaning to sit up there and watch young Trent tool his team and wagon on down into the yard, and also to keep a wary eye on those slow-riding men miles southward. He got up to the rim walking loose and easy, feeling quite alone, then he saw Rita sitting up there solemnly watching him approach, her coppery hair almost blood-red in the afternoon brightness, her violet eyes unwaveringly upon him, her heavy, ripe mouth lying closed and unsmiling.

He halted, looked at her a moment, lifted his head to look far out where Trent was coming along, dropped his eyes to her face again and eased down upon one knee, leaning upon his carbine.

She said, "I can imagine what it's like, Sloan. I watched you ride up the hill to make sure the horse went straight back to the Leonard place. Later, I watched you sit up there with your thoughts. Still later, you loped on across the draw and up the southward slope. Finally, you came up here. It's a relentless thing, isn't it?"

"What?" he asked.

"Conscience, Sloan. A man's conscience after he's killed another man."

"Yes, it's a relentless thing. But in this case the pain isn't at all the same. In this case a man feels about as he'd feel after killin' a gila monster or a rattler or a scorpion. Not at all pleased with himself—but not reproachful either."

He looked past her again. From this height it was possible to see far off towards the Moccasin Mountains. He could even see in the direction of their mustang trap, but of course he could not actually see the trap itself, only the far-away soft blur of the same country.

"Trent will have to be told," Rita said, following out Sloan's long look northward.

"That doesn't worry me, ma'am. He's big enough now to realise life's not a lantern folks turn on to make things pleasant an' turn off to make them unpleasant. What worries me is that big bunch of riders southward."

Rita looked past him briefly then back again. "I'm sorry," she murmured. "I should have explained. That's one of the cattle drives coming north to Bitterbrush Basin."

Sloan swung and slowly considered that advancing cloud of dust for a while, then he said, sounding almost disgusted with himself, "I thought it was a posse or a bunch of men Shelton Leonard might have brought on from Bidwell."

"I'm sorry, Sloan. I completely forgot you wouldn't be familiar with the drives into Bitterbrush Basin. Every spring the cowmen bring up herds and push them through Tumbleweed Pass. They return in the fall, round up, separate the different brands and head back for home again."

Sloan nodded. He'd heard this before and now, with those oncoming small figures beginning to be faintly recognisable as cattle instead of horsemen, some of his uneasiness vanished.

Rita noticed this and said, "If it had been a posse— what would you have done?"

He shrugged at her. "Depends on who might be

leadin' it. If it was a cowman-posse that maybe Shelton Leonard got up, I'd get set for trouble."

"And if it was—some other kind of a posse?"

Sloan's grey gaze went on down where Trent was making the initial long curve which would bring him around the base of the long rib of land his mother and Sloan Verrill were sitting upon.

"He'll be home in another half-hour," said Sloan, rising up and dusting his trouser-leg, then turning and offering Rita a hand up off the ground. "Reckon you'd better be thinkin' of supper and I'd better be makin' it look like I did some work around here today."

As they started down towards the buildings in their lush green, shady setting, she said, "Sloan, you can be very exasperating at times, the way you change the subject when we're talking."

"Well now, ma'am," Sloan said right back, his voice dry and drawling, "it seems to me you skirt pretty close around the thin ice yourself, now and then."

"And you don't like it when I do?"

"No, ma'am, I don't."

Rita stopped and faced around. "The only time a woman asks personal questions is when she's interested," she said, showing quick anger in her flashing gaze, then she whirled and went on down towards the ranch alone and hurrying.

Sloan kept ambling along until, in among the tree-shade again, he angled off towards the corrals. He halted once to cant a slit-eyed look up at the overhead sun. It had been several hours since the shoot-out.

Either that horse wearing Shelton Leonard's brand and bearing his dead foreman would have already arrived in Leonard's ranch-yard, or very shortly it would arrive there.

Sloan got a shovel, went out where that rotting old snubbing post stood, and went to work. It took him twenty minutes of sweat and strain to get the old post out of its earthen setting and nearly that long to set a new post in its place. By then the sun was well off in the western sky and also by then, when he listened for it, he could distinctly make out the creaking rumble of that old wagon coming up the draw.

Trent came grinding along towards the barn with a big grin for Sloan when they first saw each other. As he set the brake, looped the lines and started scrambling down he called on over into the corral where Sloan was leaning upon a tamping-bar. "They sure were hungry. When I gave 'em the hay, I think I could've gone right in among 'em. They didn't pay any attention to me at all, only the hay."

Sloan walked over and leaned upon the corral stringers. "If you had gone in among 'em, no matter how they acted to you, we'd have lost our horses and maybe you'd have wound up with a busted back."

The lad shot Sloan a grin. "I didn't go in." He worked at unharnessing and as he did so he said, "There's a cattle drive comin'. I saw the dust from up in the Pass." As he staggered under the load of harness, gave a mighty grunt and heaved it up on to the wagonbed, he said, "Sloan, we better ride out an' warn that drive not to go over an' fool around the waterhole or they'll maybe lose us our mustangs."

"Tomorrow," said Sloan, vaulting over the fence to help with the horses. "By this evenin' they might be close enough to ride down and talk to 'em. We'll keep an ear cocked. But they'll sure-enough be close enough by morning."

Trent leaned upon the pasture gate there in the pleasant shade. He looked up at the freshly-set new snubbing-post and at the un-mended broken stringers. Then he very slowly and wonderingly gazed up at Sloan in a way which did not escape the man at all.

Sloan said, "Trent, I got something to tell you. There was an interruption in the work around here today."

Trent drew out a limp bandana, wiped his perspiring face and replaced the bandana in a hip pocket. He looked out and around, then back again. He didn't say anything yet his expression said quite plainly that nothing looked any different to him there in the yard than it had for many years.

"Trent; that Juan Cortez feller came ridin' in this morning."

Now the boy's face swung upwards and his expression completely changed. In a whisper he said swiftly, "Is my maw all right?"

"Yeah, son, she's fine. But Juan Cortez is dead."

"What?" Those large, liquid soft dark blue eyes widened steadily and fixed their constant stare upon Sloan Verrill. "You killed him? You mean . . . Sloan, you telling me there was a fight here today, and you shot Juan Cortez?"

"That's about the size of it, Trent."

"Well, gosh almighty," the lad muttered, and dropped his gaze to the ground. "Tell me about it, Sloan."

"Not much to tell beyond what I've just told you. He rode in this mornin', had a few things to tell your mother, an' when I stepped out he didn't expect to see me at all."

"He thought you were with me on the wagon?"

"Yeah. He said his piece, I called him, and he wasn't fast enough."

"You buried him already?"

"Nope. Tied him over his saddle and sent him back to Mister Leonard. He sent him down here, he deserved to get him back."

Trent abruptly sat down on the grass. He looked down towards the house. He seemed suddenly to be much older than his thirteen years. "Golly, Sloan," he said very softly after the shock of Juan Cortez's passing had soaked in. "Golly."

Sloan dropped down watching the lad's profile. "I guess it had to happen," he said. "The other day, you saw how Shelton Leonard wouldn't draw against me. He sent Cortez over. Leonard didn't care which one of us walked away, son, all he wanted was that someone should determine just how fast I really am."

Trent lifted his head, round-eyed. "Juan Cortez was supposed to be the fastest gun in the Bidwell territory. I've heard the cowboys say that, Sloan. An' still, you killed him."

"It wasn't a matter of who was fastest, Trent, it was a question of who was right and who wasn't right."

"Gee, Sloan, Mister Leonard'll be madder'n a waterlogged hornet. He's got two 'breed-Indian cowboys workin' for him. They're both near as mean as Juan Cortez was too." Trent began to mournfully wag his head from side to side. "Gee whiz," he murmured. "Now you *got* to run, Sloan; now you *got* to leave the country. They'll sure kill you if they can."

Sloan got upright, cocked an eye towards the house where movement showed Rita passing over to the dinner-bell to give the plaited rope a tug, and he said, "Couldn't hardly ride on until we've got our horses in the home corral, Trent. Come on; your maw's about to ring the supper bell."

They walked slowly down towards the house and Rita, in the act of summoning them, did not ring the bell after all. She stood still and watchful as they came towards her. Sloan saw that she'd changed to a gunpowder-blue dress that deepened and darkened the violet shade of her eyes. He also saw that she was looking sombrely out at him, so he inclined his head to silently convey the meaning to her that he had informed Trent of Juan Cortez's killing.

Rita understood. She stopped her son before he went past, and softly said, "Honey, we owe Mister Verrill a big debt. If he hadn't shot Cortez I'm afraid to imagine when you came back home this afternoon, what you'd have found."

"But, maw," said Trent in a voice gone shrill with dismay. "They'll kill him now. Mister Leonard'll send those 'breed cowboys of his over here and. . . ." Trent broke off to make a helpless gesture and look up into his mother's face. She shook her head at him.

"I don't think the odds against Sloan will be that big, Trent. There'll be you and me standing with him, won't there?"

Trent's face suddenly brightened. He swung towards Sloan with his eyes shining. "Sure," he crowed. "Sure, Sloan; I near forgot. We're pardners anyway, aren't we, an' pardners stand together."

Over the lad's head his mother and durable Sloan Verrill exchanged a long look.

TWELVE

IT was nearly eight o'clock with supper long over and the good scent of approaching nightfall thickening around the ranch when Sloan heard horsemen coming in from the murky east. He was with Trent and Rita on the front porch of the mainhouse when he heard those shod hooves, but as alert as he was Trent sprang up first.

"Someone's coming," said the boy breathlessly, and spun towards the door.

"Whoa," called over Sloan. "Where you goin'?"

"To get the Winchester. It'll probably be Mister Leonard an' his cowboys, Sloan."

Rita got up from her chair also. She didn't say anything but faint starshine showed how tight and troubled her expression was.

Sloan stood up, cocked his head to listen a moment, then said to the lad, "This isn't Leonard's way, son. He'll probably come all right, but not ridin' right up to the front door like this."

"I'll fetch the Winchester anyway," said Trent, and reached for the door.

"No," said Sloan. "You never mind that carbine. Just take your maw indoors and keep an ear skinned."

Rita went dutifully over and took her son's arm. When he would have protested she tightened her grip. Those two passed on out of sight into the house where only one lamp burned, and that was out in the kitchen.

Sloan stepped down from the porch, walked out almost to the hitchrack and moved over into cottonwood-shadows there. He could now make out the shapes and silhouettes of two riders as they came slouching along towards the house. He heard one man say the place was dark, and the other cowboy say no, there was a light around back.

Both riders halted at the rack, looked around, then swung down. That was when Sloan stepped forth. The cowboys saw him and stood stock-still as he advanced towards them.

"'Evenin'," he drawled, his voice quietly soft and non-committal.

"'Evenin'," the taller and older-looking of the strange riders said back, with a little, sharp chop of his head up and down. "We're with the Henderson drive.

Come up to within a couple miles of here this after-noon an' rode on ahead to see how Miz' Drummond an' her boy are."

Sloan leaned upon the rack studying those two. That older man was steady-eyed and rough looking. He was long, lanky, and sinewy with the eternal youth some men had built into them. The other cowboy was much younger and of medium height, but of the two, this one stared longest and hardest at Sloan.

"She's in the house," Sloan said. "Go on up, if you want."

The cowboys exchanged a wooden look; something passed back and forth between them. Sloan saw that look, thought he understood it and felt dark blood rising into his face as the taller and older man said, "Yeah; reckon I'll do that."

Sloan and the younger cowboy stood awkwardly behind as the lanky man strode off through gathering dusk. The younger man said, with elaborate casual-ness, "Every springtime when we come north with the drive, we stop by an' see does Miz' Drummond need anythin' from town, 'cause we usually send the wagon to town after we get settled over in the Basin."

"Right decent of you," drawled Sloan, beginning to feel amused at the very obvious curiosity upon the cowboy's face.

"You work for her, stranger?" asked the cowboy, making this question sound as casual as he could.

"Well, I reckon you could call it that," answered Sloan.

The younger man stepped up closer, fished in a pocket for his tobacco sack, dropped his head and went to work twisting up a cigarette. When he lit up he offered Sloan the makings, got a refusal and put the things back into his pocket. As he exhaled and gazed towards the house where his friend was softly talking to someone at the doorway, he said, "You know, stranger, if I'd figured she'd needed a man around, danged if I wouldn't have come up lookin' for the job myself."

Sloan's gaze turned gradually hard and knowing. He didn't know this cowboy at all, had never before seen him in fact, but he knew the man's type and now he also knew how the cowboy's thoughts were running.

"Would you have?" he said softly.

"Yes, sir. She's a mighty handsome woman, stranger. Some fellers have all the luck."

"Mind makin' that a little plainer?" Sloan asked, beginning to draw upright where he'd been leaning upon the hitchrack.

The cowboy exhaled a big bluish cloud. His teeth shone whitely in the dusk and his eyes dropped to Sloan's face. "You don't need a picture, do you?" he asked.

Sloan's fist came out of nowhere, exploded with the sound of a distant pistol-shot, and the young cowboy went over backwards, his hat flying in one direction, his half-smoked cigarette in another direction.

Sloan stepped around the rack, walked over and trod out the cigarette, blew on his knuckles and was standing there gazing quietly upon the unconscious man when his lanky companion returned. Standing silhouetted upon the porch sixty feet away was Rita Drummond.

Sloan turned as the older cowboy halted and gazed stonily down at his companion. The lanky man drew in a big breath and let it out, he then waggled his head back and forth. Without any animosity he said quietly, "Never fails; always got to be one clown to make wise remarks." He glanced over at Sloan. "That was it, wasn't it?"

Sloan nodded.

The tall man thumbed back his hat, put a critical look downwards and wondered aloud how long it would be before his pardner would come around.

Sloan had no estimate to make. He faced the other man, saw the steady, cold appraisal in those faded old eyes, and waited. The older man was curious too, but since he'd lived longer he was not going to take any chances on a stranger who might be yeasty with temper and prickly with pride.

"Got a smoke?" he asked. Sloan shook his head again, knelt and regarded the fallen man. He had his back to the tall man. The younger cowboy groaned and writhed as consciousness began returning. Sloan got back upright and dusted his knees.

He said: "I reckon everyone's got to make that mistake at least once, before he grows up."

The tall cowboy gravely inclined his head. "The trouble is, stranger, sometimes they don't just get off with a sore jaw."

Sloan turned, regarded the gloomy look on the other man's craggy, weathered features and felt a kindling liking for him. "He didn't mean anything," Sloan said. "All he needed was a little lesson. I reckon you and I were long on lip an' short on brains at his age too."

"Yeah," assented the tall man, watching his friend flop over, climb unsteadily to one knee and hang there shaking his head. "You got quite a wallop, Mister Verrill."

The sound of his name in that lanky rangerider's voice told Sloan a lot. Rita had mentioned Juan Cortez; he knew without being told that this was so; knew it from the carefully thoughtful way the older man was talking and acting, and also from the wondering way this older man looked at him.

Sloan drawled, "I don't think it was the wallop so much as it was his glass jaw."

"That could be," agreed the lanky cowboy, speaking clinically and detachedly. "One time down in Carson City he got dropped like this, an' I swear the feller who done it didn't weigh a hundred and thirty pounds with rocks in his socks."

The older man stooped, caught his friend by the arm and hoisted him upright. That younger rider put up a hand, gingerly explored his jaw wobbling it back and forth to make certain it was not broken, and as his eyes cleared he focused his entire attention upon Sloan. Finally, with both legs wide set, he shook off the solicitous hand of his pardner and glared.

"You damned louse," he said thickly to Sloan. "You took me off guard. Let's see you try that again, you doggoned. . . ."

"Easy, Matt," soothed his pardner. "You had it coming."

"Go to hell," growled the younger man, squaring fully around towards Sloan Verrill and dropping his right hand straight down.

"Matt," said the older man quietly, almost casually. "You're teeterin' on the edge of Eternity, boy. This here is Sloan Verrill."

"What of it?" snarled the young cowboy, his eyes blazing. "Who the hell is Sloan Verrill?"

"He's the feller who shot it out with Juan Cortez this mornin'—and killed him."

The young cowboy's expression very slowly and gradually altered. He swung his eyes finally and stared hard at his pardner, as though he wasn't sure he'd heard right. "Killed Juan Cortez. . . ?"

"Yep. Face to face."

Sloan kept watching the younger man. It became amply plain that as the killer of the renowned Shelton Leonard's gunfighting rangeboss, Sloan had projected himself into a position of unexcelled, unquestioned, superiority in the Bitterbrush Basin country.

Matt let his shoulders ease off, let his stance loosen its bristling stiffness, and turned his round-eyed look back to Sloan again. "That true?" he asked softly, almost in a whisper. "You shot it out with Juan Cortez, mister?"

Instead of answering Sloan stepped up closer and held out his hand. "If you still want to offer me your tobacco," he said, "I'd sure be grateful."

The sack came out and was wordlessly passed over. Both those riders watched Sloan as he made his smoke, lit it and passed back the makings. He exhaled, looked out and around, saw Rita still over there in the porch-shadows, and said, "Yeah. Cortez second, Shelton Leonard first. Only Leonard wouldn't draw, so we had it out hand-to-hand."

The young cowboy made a long, audible sigh. His taller, older pardner worked up a frown and said, "Mister Verrill; you sure don't fool around with the second-best ones, do you? Leonard'll be after your scalp, an' he won't rest until he gets it. I reckon a real smart man would sort of saddle up in the night and put a heap of miles under him before sunup."

Sloan said, lifting his cigarette, "I never was very smart, I guess. Anyway, runnin' from someone like Leonard doesn't solve anything. If he doesn't pick on me he'll pick on someone else. His kind's like that."

"You don't have to tell us anything about Shelton Leonard," said the older man dryly. "We've been bringin' cattle up to Bitterbrush Basin for a long time, and nearly every cussed year he gives us some kind of trouble."

"And you take it?" asked Sloan, eyeing the older man with a look of mild surprise on his face. This rugged, rawhide-tough older man didn't look like a person who would take much pushing around.

116

But the older rider merely shrugged, saying nothing. His friend though had an explanation to offer. He hooked both thumbs in his shell-belt and said, "This here is Pat Dougherty, Mister Verrill. He's my paw's trail boss. I'm Matt Henderson." Matt paused, licked his lips and made a sheepish little lopsided grin. "I got to apologise. I had that crack on the jaw comin'."

"Forget it," Sloan murmured, with a faint twinkle in his gaze. "I might've been a mite touchy tonight."

"Well; it's over an' done with anyway, Mister Verrill," said young Henderson as he gently touched his sore jaw. "Anyway, my paw owns that herd we brought up today, an' he won't let any of us get into a brawl with Leonard. He says we'd be layin' ourselves wide open to serious loss if we did that, because after we settle the critters over into the Basin an' pull out for the home ranch, Leonard and his riders are the only ones left up here. Paw says it's better to eat a little crow then to maybe wind up getting five, six thousand dollars worth of critters run off or stampeded or maybe even poisoned."

"I see that Leonard's got an upstandin' reputation," exclaimed Sloan.

Pat Dougherty strolled over to his horse, un-looped his reins and turned the animal preparatory to mounting. Over one shoulder he said, "Mister Verrill; if I was you I'd sure develop an eye in the back of my head."

Young Matt Henderson also mounted up. He felt his jaw again and appraisingly considered Sloan. "I know about how Leonard felt after you hit him," he said, and smiled. "Well, Mister Verrill, we'd like to come by tomorrow an' fill our water barrels at the pump if you folks don't mind. Drummond always used to let us do that when he was alive."

"Sure," said Sloan. "If it's all right with Mrs. Drummond I sure got no objection. And Matt—you got a friend here as long as I'm around, swollen jaw or not."

Pat Dougherty smiled for the first time. "I got a feelin' you two might need each other at that," he said, reining around. "See you tomorrow, Mister Verrill."

Sloan stood out by the rack watching as those two riders passed slowly back down the star-brightened night. He had his back to Rita so she couldn't see it, but he was grinning. Young Matt Henderson had learned a lesson this night, and because he wasn't a vindictive type, he'd not forget it right away, nor bear a grudge either. That was one thing about open-range cowboys; they were rarely educated in the sense of more civilised people, but what lessons they learned they usually had very good reason to remember.

"Sloan. . . ?"

He turned and slow-paced on up to where Rita stood on the porch. She would want to know what had happened out by the hitchrack, and for once it didn't irritate him to think of facing that curiosity.

THIRTEEN

P AT DOUGHERTY came by in the cool morning with one of the three wagons accompanying the Henderson herd. While two big-eyed, silent cowboys eyed Sloan, Dougherty explained that they had their water kegs along. Sloan led them around to the pump, left the two cowboys filling barrels while he and Dougherty walked over into cottonwood shade at the older man's suggestion.

"Listen," Dougherty said, the moment they were alone. "Shelton Leonard come by the camp last night on his way to Bidwell. He told us you bushwhacked Juan Cortez, shot him in the back, and he was goin' for the law."

Sloan digested this while watching young Trent walk purposefully over to the barn and disappear inside. "Leonard's no fool," he mused aloud. "He undoubtedly buried Cortez by now, so there'll be no proof I didn't shoot him in the back."

"Yeah," said Dougherty, "but Miz' Drummond told me last night she seen the whole thing an' it was face-to-face and plumb fair. She'd be a witness in your favour, man."

Sloan nodded agreement with this but his anxious expression did not lessen. Leonard did not actually know how his gunfighting rangeboss had died. He was not there when the fight took place, did not know anyone else was there, and yet he was going to ride sixty miles to bring back the law to arrest Sloan Verrill.

"He's no fool," said Verrill. "He wouldn't go to all this trouble unless he was damned sure he could bring it off."

"How?" Dougherty asked.

"I don't know," said Sloan candidly. "Maybe I'd better ride over and see if I can get anything out of his riders."

"A bullet is more'n likely what you'll get," said Pat Dougherty dryly. "Mister Verrill, if it's the same two 'breed riders he's had the past four, five years, believe me they'll shoot first and from behind somethin', then they'll come out an' see who they shot."

"Got to risk it," mumbled Sloan, and raised troubled eyes to the taller, older man. "Dougherty, you could do me a big favour. Trent Drummond and I got a wild-horse trap out at a waterhole in Bitterbrush Basin. We trapped about forty critters an' since I won't be able to go out and rope or hobble the best critters and line 'em out for the home-place today, like I told Trent I'd do, I wonder if I could pay you an' maybe one or two Henderson men to go out with the boy an' take care of that job for me?"

"You trapped mustangs in Bitterbrush Basin?" asked Dougherty with a round-eyed look. "An' you got forty head of 'em corralled out there now?" Dougherty elaborately wagged his head back and forth. "Be damned," he mumbled, and in a louder voice: "Be *double* damned! A dozen fellers have tried it an' to-date haven't any of 'em ever trapped a single horse out there. Sure, Mister Verrill, sure enough; I'll go back, get hold of Matt and another feller, take the lad an' we'll go out and see what you got."

Sloan took down his bridle, went out into the pasture, caught his bay horse and rigged him out over in the shade by the gate. There, as he was finishing up, young Trent came over looking puzzled.

"Hey, Sloan, Mister Dougherty just told me you wouldn't be able to go out to the trap today."

"That's right," replied the older man, turning to face the boy. "I got another little chore that's got to be done. But the Henderson riders are goin' out to do the ropin' and hobblin', Trent. But you'll have to go with 'em an' pick out the best horses."

The boy's eyes clouded up with indecision. "Gee, Sloan, I don't know as I'd know which were the best ones. I'm not real good at—"

"What? Why of course you'd know the best ones. And listen, pardner, when they line out those hobbled critters to drive 'em back here, you be cussed sure not to get too close to 'em. A hobbled horse may not be able to run or strike, but don't ever think he can't be dangerous."

Sloan stepped up over leather, caught movement on ahead beyond the Henderson wagon where Rita had come out of the house, and abruptly reined away. He twisted to gaze back once, just before passing out of sight up through the trees along the creek-bank. Young Trent was standing back there perplexedly watching him. Sloan grinned and threw back a careless wave.

He let his animal pick its own trail and gait as far as the westerly rim, and up there he halted to gaze back down into the Drummond yard. Pat Dougherty and the others were down by the Henderson wagon; from that height they seemed very small and insignificant.

Sloan took his time at studying the roundabout country. There was nothing to be seen over in Bitter-brush Basin, nor on westward either, but south-east-ward was the great sprawl and dust of a big cattle herd getting under way for the final leg of the drive on through Tumbleweed Pass.

Sloan did not know this westward country so he rode it carefully and warily. He spotted potential bush-whacking sites and detoured wide around them. He also saw cattle after he'd covered three or four miles and was well into Shelton Leonard's range, but every head he could get close to bore the identical zig-zag brand which he read as a lightning streak, and search as he might he could find no critters which appeared to have re-worked marks on them.

It was near noon when he came out around a low landswell and sighted ranch buildings a mile ahead. He drew back out of sight, dismounted, took his car-bine and climbed to the crest of the landswell, lay up there for a half-hour watching for signs of activity among those buildings, and finally saw it.

There was a man down there in the ranch yard who appeared to be aimlessly wandering back and forth. A guard, Sloan thought. Whatever Shelton Leonard was up to, he'd left one of his riders to guard the ranch while he was making his ride down to Bidwell.

Sloan wondered where the other cowboy was, and he lay still with hot sunlight punishing him atop that exposed ridge trying to catch sight of a second man. He never did; if that other rider was down there at the ranch, he was keeping out of sight.

Sloan considered the best way to approach those buildings. There was no way to get down there without being seen unless he crept afoot through the brush, and even that was unlikely to prove successful because, with admirable foresight, someone had cleared away all brush for a quarter mile around those onward buildings.

He went back to his horse, stepped up and reined on around the landswell riding straight for the buildings. This was, he felt, the best way to get over there. He would of course be seen by that sentry down there, but there was no alternative unless he wished to await nightfall, which he had no intention of doing.

As he rode through the bright sunlight he kept an intent watch upon the visible man down there among the buildings, but what kept him uneasy was the certain knowledge that there was another man somewhere around.

It was possible that Leonard had sent that second rider off somewhere on the range to do some kind of work; perhaps clean a waterhole or hunt some stray cattle. If this were so, then Sloan would have only that onward man to contend with. But if it were not so, if

Leonard had put that second rider to also guarding the ranch, but out a ways and perhaps on horseback, then there was an excellent chance Sloan would be in that man's sights as he approached the ranch.

This was a chance he had to take, so, riding as cannily as he could, avoiding all the places where an ambusher could be lying in wait, he kept right on pacing along towards the buildings.

He was still well beyond rifle-range when he saw that guard down there suddenly step out into the yard facing east and stand there gazing straight out at him. The man's very erect, very still stance, said plainly enough that he had sighted Sloan. Abruptly, the guard spun about, ran over to the barn, jumped inside that old weathered building and re-emerged carrying a Winchester saddle-gun.

Sloan made a calculation and when he thought he was almost within range he halted, lifted his hand and made a palm-out gesture with it, indicating that he came in peace.

The cowboy down in the yard saw this but he did not respond to it with a similar gesture, instead, he stood there watching Sloan with his whole attention, gripping that Winchester in both hands.

Sloan took a long chance. He knew that guard did not know him by sight. So far he had only seen two of the men from the Leonard ranch, and one of them was dead while the other one, Shelton Leonard, was a long way off by now on his way to Bidwell.

He reached for his pocket-watch, palmed it and held

up his hand so that bright sunlight reflected off the watch case. He called forward to that tense, armed man on ahead. "It's the law. We heard there's trouble over here. I came out to investigate. All right to ride on in?"

The cowboy did not reply right away but he grounded his carbine and leaned upon it. He was a tall, powerfully put-together man with a dark face and suspicious way of staring. Finally he called back in a rumbling voice: "Yeah; ride on in."

Sloan put away his watch; he was confident at that distance the cowboy had been quite unable to ascertain that the shiny thing he'd held up had not been a badge. His horse moved out, walking slowly along, and Sloan kept searching among those onward buildings for the second man he felt sure would not be too far away even if he wasn't there in the yard.

The last hundred yards he concentrated upon the dark man, who was also concentrating upon Sloan. To implement the deception, Sloan started talking as he entered the yard.

"We got word day before yesterday over in Bidwell there was some trouble over here. Supposed to have been a fight or somethin' between Shelton Leonard an' some stranger who came down the Tumbleweed Trail. The marshal thought someone ought to ride out an' take a look at this stranger. There's been a lot of activity lately along the hootowl trails; he thought this stranger might be one of these here wanted men."

He reined up thirty feet away from the dark-eyed

cowboy and made a casual survey of the yard. "Where's Mister Leonard?"

The cowboy loosened, his appraisal over and done with. In a voice showing no suspicion he said, "Gone over to Bidwell to see the sheriff. You two must've passed one another."

"No," said Sloan, "I didn't see a soul. Maybe he went farther south than I did. I hit the Drummond place this morning."

"Yeah? Well, that's where the stranger's stayin'."

Sloan made a frown. "Didn't see any stranger down there," he said, giving the Indian-looking cowboy a long stare. "Saw Miz' Drummond; she said she didn't know anything about any trouble around here."

The 'breed cowboy made a derisive snort. "She was lyin', Deputy. If you want proof get down an' come along. I'll show you something."

Sloan rode on over to the hitchrack in front of the barn, swung down, looped his reins and waited until the big 'breed ambled up, beckoned, and hiked on over to a small dilapidated shed set off by itself a hundred yards from the other buildings.

The 'breed halted at this small building, propped his carbine against the wall, fumbled for a key and unlocked the door. As he stepped inside he looked back and jerked his head for Sloan to also enter. Sloan did; it was pitch-dark and clammy in the shed, which had thick, insulated walls and had evidently at one time been a storehouse for provisions.

There was a rickety, long table in the centre of the

shed. The cowboy groped around, found a candle, lit it and held it high as he said, indicating a mound of canvas on the table, "Strip back the canvas, Deputy."

Sloan stepped forth, lifted the canvas, and found himself staring into the sightless face of Juan Cortez. He scowled; it was not difficult to seem surprised either. He had thought Leonard would have buried the dead gunfighter.

The cowboy stepped up, gave the canvas a tug, and exposed Cortez's upper body. He gripped the corpse firmly and rolled it half over exposing Cortez's back. There were two unmistakable bullet holes between the dead Mexican's shoulder-blades.

Triumphantly the 'breed cowboy said, "Bush-whacked, Deputy. There's the proof. Two slugs in the back."

Sloan breathed softly, "I'll be damned," and he wasn't play-acting at all.

The 'breed carelessly flung the canvas back over Cortez and swung black eyes to Sloan's face. He smiled, evidently impressed by the look of astonishment he saw. "It was that stranger hidin' out over at the Drummond place."

"You sure?" Sloan asked, beginning to understand what Leonard was attempting to do.

"We're sure all right," replied the 'breed, turning back towards the door with his high-held candle. "Mister Leonard seen that stranger sneak out from behind some rocks and pot-shoot Cortez. Saw it plain as day. That's why he lit out for Bidwell to fetch back a posse an' have that damned outlaw arrested. It was murder plain as day."

The cowboy set down his candle-stub, blew it out and stepped aside for Sloan to pass on out of the shed ahead of him. "We got Cortez's gun up at the house. It hasn't been fired."

Sloan stepped outside in the sunlight and thoughtfully considered the big 'breed's back as the cowboy turned to re-lock the shed door. "How'd Mister Leonard happen to be handy when the stranger killed Cortez?" he asked.

"Sound carries in this country," explained the 'breed. "He heard the first shot. He was just over the ridge. Him and Cortez was out huntin' strays together. He rode up over the rim an' seen that feller shoot Cortez the second time." As the 'breed turned away he was smiling again. "Sure wish you'd crossed trails with Mister Leonard," he said. "It'd have saved him a heap of ridin'."

FOURTEEN

SLOAN walked back over into the shade of Shelton Leonard's old barn with the half-Indian cowboy. He was sombre and silent, which the big 'breed evidently believed was from the gravity of that recent disclosure of pure murder.

The 'breed set his Winchester against the barn wall, felt around in his vest pockets for the makings, and leaned there with his shoulders against the barn-wall as he went to work manufacturing a cigarette. He still wore that triumphant, faint smile.

Sloan sank down upon a handy horseshoe keg, pushed back his hat and gazed out over the empty land. It was fairly clear what Leonard had done. He'd pumped two bullets into Juan Cortez's corpse when the dead gunfighter's horse had brought him back to Leonard's ranch. He'd pumped those two slugs into Cortez to support his contention that Sloan Verrill had murdered his foreman. And now he was on his way to Bidwell for the law, and again, his purpose was transparent. With Cortez's back-shot corpse to prove his accusation that the Mexican had been murdered, Leonard could count on the law to do to Verrill what neither he nor Juan Cortez had been able to do.

It was a clever and deadly scheme, and if Sloan hadn't ridden over to the Leonard ranch he'd never have known how well Shelton Leonard had framed his neck into a hangrope.

The cowboy lit up and blew a cloud of smoke downward as he gazed at Sloan, still faintly smiling. "Sort of surprised you, didn't it?" he said. "It sure surprised us fellers too. In fact Mister Leonard set me to keepin' watch over the ranch until he gets back with a posse, just in case that gunslingin' outlaw decides to try an' wipe us all out, with his bushwhackin' ways."

Sloan said flatly, "You the only rider Leonard's still got workin' for him?"

"No," replied the big 'breed. "There's another hand. Mister Leonard sent him over into Bitterbrush Basin today. Seems this here killer's went and built a mustang trap over there at the waterhole an' Mister Leonard sent him to tear it down."

Sloan looked around. "Why?"

"That's the only waterhole that ain't alkali for a long ways. He's got no right fencin' it off."

"You fellers got cattle in the Basin?"

"No, but as soon as Mister Leonard gets back we will have. He always turns out over in the Basin this time of the year."

"Yeah," murmured Sloan, getting to his feet. "On my way in I saw a big herd comin' out of the south."

The 'breed's gaze turned suddenly sharp and interested. "Know whose drive it might be?" he asked.

Sloan made an indifferent shrug. "Henderson maybe. I didn't get close enough to make positive identification but it looked like some of Henderson's riders out on the wings."

The 'breed smoked and scowled and said no more for a while. He was obviously turning something over in his mind. For as long as this quiet interval ran on, Sloan was also busy with some private thoughts. He finally slapped his leg, looked over at his drowsing mount and said, "Suppose I deputise you," he said to the 'breed cowboy, "and the pair of us go down to the Drummond place and make a stab at takin' that gunfighter down there."

The 'breed's muddy black gaze turned bleakly disapproving. "Not on your life," he said. "That feller's lightning with a gun. You saw what he done to Juan

Cortez, and Juan was known as the fastest gun for a hundred. . . ."

"But that was in the back," said Sloan, watching the cowboy's face.

The 'breed paused, thought a moment, then looked slightly abashed, as though he'd almost said something he shouldn't have. "Back or front, I figure my job is to guard the ranch like Mister Leonard told me to."

"Maybe I'll ride down there an' try it by myself, then. If I keep my badge out of sight he won't jump me—maybe."

"The hell he won't," boomed the big 'breed. "Miz' Drummond talked to you, an' she'll tell that killer who you are before you even get into the yard."

"Maybe he's run out by now," suggested Sloan. This seemed to give the 'breed something to think about, so Sloan followed it up by saying, "Outlaws don't usually hang around once they know the law's on the trail. Hell; instead of ridin' on over here today, maybe I should've hung around the Drummond place instead, because if he's left the country it's goin' to take a heap more ridin' to find him again."

"Be a hell of a note if he *did* make a run for it," muttered the 'breed. "Mister Leonard'll be madder'n a wet hen, when he gets back with a posse, and that killer's plumb gone."

The Indian fidgeted. He turned an annoyed look at Sloan. "Why'n hell did you go an' tell Miz' Drummond who you were?"

"I had no idea there was an outlaw at her place. The way we got the rumour down in Bidwell was that. . . ."

"It's done anyway," broke in the 'breed, looking increasingly bothered by the prospect of that supposed outlaw over at the Drummond ranch escaping. "Hell; I wish Mister Leonard was here. Or even Frank—our other rider. Then a couple of us could ride on down there with you."

"We don't need more'n just you'n me," said Sloan.

But the big 'breed was adamant about this and sternly shook his head. "I dassen't leave," he growled. "But even if I could, just the two of us wouldn't be enough gunpower against that feller."

Sloan pushed forward, went over and halted beside his horse, freed the reins and turned to thoughtfully regard the cowboy. "Think I'll just ride up atop that westerly rim above the Drummond place and keep watch." He toed in, stepped up and settled down across leather. "If Leonard left for Bidwell last night, he won't be back at the quickest before tomorrow."

"More'n like the day after," opined the 'breed from over in front of the barn. "It's a long ride there and back."

Sloan nodded and looked over where that little forlorn shed was, with Cortez's body inside it. He made a little head-wag saying quietly, "Why would that outlaw shoot Cortez?"

The 'breed lifted his gaze, hung it upon Sloan's face and shrugged. "Maybe he's just a killer. Maybe Cortez caught him at something."

"What did Mister Leonard say about that?"

Another shrug from the 'breed. "All he said was that he seen the killer fire that second slug into Cortez's back as Juan was fallin' off his horse, shot down from behind."

"But there has to be a reason."

The cowboy was not interested. "Cortez is dead," he said simply. "Shot down from behind. Don't much else matter, Deputy. Murder is murder."

"Did you look in his wallet?" asked Sloan.

The Indian shook his head. "Mister Leonard took his gun and stuff up to the house."

Sloan nodded over this but kept staring over at that little shed. Finally he said, "Let's go have another look."

The Indian was not interested. He fished around for the shed-key, found it and tossed it up to Sloan. "Go look if you want," he muttered. "I'm gettin' hungry. I'll be over at the cook-shack if you want me."

Sloan waited until the big 'breed had sauntered indifferently on across the yard, then rode over to that little shed, got down, unlocked the door and entered. He wasn't in there more than a minute, though. He re-locked the door, left the key in its lock, stepped back up over his horse and reined on out of Shelton Leonard's ranch yard riding slowly.

He thought the 'breed cowboy might be watching, so he took his time as far as that distant landswell. But once he got around behind that and was shielded from sight, he booted his horse over into a long lope heading north-eastward. He was remembering what the 'breed had told him about Leonard's other cowboy being out in Bitterbrush Basin. He was certain that if that other cowboy got to the mustang trap and encountered several Henderson riders out there, he would do nothing. But there was also a chance that Leonard's man might have arrived at the trap *ahead* of young Trent and the others; if that had occurred, he could guess what Leonard's man had done by now—turned all their horses loose and torn down their trap.

But when he came to a sharp lift in the onward land he swerved his horse and rode to the top of it. He meant to use this as a lookout, but not entirely in the direction of Bitterbrush Basin.

He dismounted, walked over into some oak-tree shade and leaned there looking back down the way he'd just come. There was nothing but an endless, hushed, sun-dappled expanse of emptiness beneath a faded, azure sky. Still, Sloan stood there waiting and watching, and eventually he saw what he'd hoped to sight.

At first there was only one small puff of smoke. But within minutes a steady straight-standing thick gauze-like pillar of smoke rose up from far back where the Leonard ranch was. Gradually that smoke turned dark and turgid as though impelled upwards by furiously crackling licks of flame. Sloan could not see the flames but he knew they were beneath all that smoke, and he smiled. If Shelton Leonard was wily enough to put two back-shots into a corpse in order to frame

Sloan Verrill for murder, then the least Sloan could do was match Leonard with a trick of his own.

When he'd visited the shed holding Cortez's body the last time, he'd simply lit that tallow-candle and had locked the door leaving it burning inside that tinder-dry place. There wouldn't be enough left of Juan Cortez now for anyone to show the lawmen from Bidwell, and the slaying of Leonard's gunfighting rangeboss was right back where it had originally been—in the realm of justified killing.

Sloan got back astride, eased down off the oak-knoll and continued on his way in the general direction of Tumbleweed Pass and Bitterbrush Basin. He sighted dust near the southern terminus of the Pass while he was still a mile off, and angled along the slopes to come in where that dust was being made. He still had in mind that other cowboy of Shelton Leonard's, the one supposedly over in Bitterbrush Basin somewhere.

But when he got close enough to look down where the Pass ran out southerly, he saw six or seven riders, including a shockle-headed young lad, and scuffling along ahead of them making that dust, some nearly exhausted mustangs in wrapped hobbles.

The animals had fought hard; there were skinned places on every one of them, bruises and bumps and dried blood. But a hobbled horse never learnt about hobbles by fighting them, he learned about them by experience. These horses had had over five miles to realise this. They had thrown themselves, fallen, reared up and come down on their sides, but five miles later the wiser ones among them had learned the bitter truth; like it or not they were captured and at the mercy of the men around them—plus the figure-eight Mormon hobbles around their ankles. Fighting was futile, so they stopped resisting after a few miles and by the time Sloan saw them, they were crow-hopping along in their hobbles as though they were old, seasoned hands at travelling like this.

Sloan angled down off the easterly slope, swung into the trail and sat easy waiting for the other riders to come up. When they did he saw young Trent's blinding smile among the men. He also recognised young Matt Henderson and rugged old Pat Dougherty. The others were Henderson cowboys who obviously had ridden along for the fun of it, and while these men did not know Sloan Verrill, they smiled at him anyway; as the slayer of renowned gunslinger Juan Cortez he commanded a good deal of respect.

Trent pushed on up, reined old Bally down and waved an arm at the large band of horses. "We got 'em trail-broke, Sloan, but golly, I had no idea it'd be so hard to up-end 'em and get the hobbles on. If it hadn't been for Mister Matt an' Mister Pat I don't think we'd ever have got it done."

Dougherty came up, dropped his rein-hand and looked straight over Trent's head, his eyes asking an obvious question. Sloan returned that look briefly, dropped his eyes to Trent and said, "How many'd you pick out, pardner?"

"Forty-seven, Sloan."

"Good. Tell you what, Trent. You dust it on ahead and open the corral gates. All right?"

"Sure, Sloan. See you at the ranch."

Dougherty and Verrill watched the lad gallop away southward. Without taking his eyes off Trent's diminishing form Dougherty said, "What'd you learn over there?"

Also watching young Trent, Sloan said, "The damndest thing you ever saw. They hadn't buried Cortez. They had him in a shed over there to show the sheriff. He had two bullet-holes in his back; fresh bullet-holes put there after he was dead, but convincin' enough to come awful close to gettin' me hanged."

"I figured Leonard wouldn't make that sixty-mile ride to town unless he had something worked out real good," exclaimed Dougherty. "Well; what you figure to do?"

Sloan twisted in the saddle, lifted an arm and pointed. "See that smoke?" he said. "Well; I already did it. I burnt down the shack where Leonard was keeping Cortez."

Dougherty considered that smoke for a while, looped his reins and began to make a smoke. After a while, when the others had gone on past and the dust was settling, back in their wake, Dougherty said, "Mister Verrill, one of Leonard's riders was watchin' us line out these wild horses today. He kept skulkin' far out, but I know that one. His name's Frank Cosineau. He's a bad 'breed. For a hundred dollars cash he'd ambush his own mother. Now that you burnt up Leonard's chance to have the law do his dirty work for him, you watch your back-trail real close—real close. Unless I miss my guess a country mile, Leonard'll put Frank Cosineau on your trail now."

FIFTEEN

IT was late afternoon before they got the mustangs corralled at the Drummond place, and as Sloan Verrill came riding up with rugged Pat Dougherty at his side a grizzled, wiry, older man with faded, rock-hard eyes and a drooping Longhorn moustache sauntered over to gaze upon Sloan as the younger man dismounted. This was old Eli Henderson, the father of young Matt and the owner of the big Henderson herd which was scattered now on across Bitterbrush Basin. He extended a work-roughened hand, saying, "I've heard quite a little about you, Mister Verrill," and as Sloan gripped that hand and pumped it, the old cowman, with a sardonic twinkle said, "I've also seen your handiwork—on my son's jaw."

Sloan dropped old Henderson's hand and gazed into the older man's eyes. "Well, I reckon that was a sort of a mistake," he said.

Eli Henderson shook his head. "No; I kind of doubt that it was any mistake. Matt's young; he's got a lot to learn. I'm grateful you used your fist instead of your gun. Matt's a good boy."

Pat Dougherty cocked an eye at old Henderson. "Tell him about Leonard's scheme," he said to Sloan,

138

and Verrill complied, explaining to Eli Henderson how Shelton Leonard had planned to make a murderer out of him. The old cowman listened, showed no surprise at all, and ran the back of one hand under his shaggy old drooping moustache.

"Shelton Leonard's no good," he said quietly. "I've known him nearly twenty years. He's a rustler an' a killer, but no one's ever been able to prove any of it. I'm not surprised he worked up something like this, Mister Verrill, and I'll be real surprised if he lets it end with the destruction of his evidence against you."

"I already warned him about Cosineau," put in Dougherty, and turned as young Matt Henderson strolled up beating dust from his trousers with his hat. "Get 'em all corralled?" Dougherty asked Matt. The younger man nodded, threw a smile and a nod over at Verrill, and twisted to look over where the Henderson riders were lining the corral looking in at the shaggy, sweaty, wild-eyed horses.

"Kind of late today to take the hobbles off 'em," Matt said. "Maybe we'd better just let 'em stiffen up tonight and set 'em free tomorrow."

Eli Henderson ignored this; he clearly had something else on his mind. To Sloan he said, "You figurin' on stayin' in the country, Mister Verrill?"

Sloan nodded, gazing straight at the old cowman.

"Good," exclaimed Henderson. "I got a proposition for you. I usually have to send a couple of men up here two or three times each summer to salt, and sort of look after the cattle. When Drummond was alive I paid him to do this for me. Now then, if you'd be interested, I'd be right glad to pay you to watch the cattle and do a little saltin'."

Sloan, not expecting anything like this, dropped his gaze and stood thoughtfully turning this proposition over in his mind. It was Pat Dougherty who broke the silence after it had run on for a while, by saying, "Mister Henderson give Drummond a choice of takin' his pay in cash or cattle. Drummond took cattle."

Sloan looked up at Pat. "That's where he got that thirty head, then. Right?"

Old Eli nodded. "Yeah; I let him pick his own cows in the fall of the year. Give him fifteen head for a summer's work. After two summers he had thirty head of real good heifers."

"They're gone," said Sloan simply. Dougherty and the two Hendersons exchanged a guarded look, then the old man tugged on his moustache, wrinkled his lined forehead and looked over at the house.

"Not much a lone female can do in country like this, Mister Verrill," he said. "It's a big land and it's rough. When a widow-woman's got a neighbour like Shelton Leonard I reckon she can count herself lucky if all she loses is her thirty cows."

Sloan also looked around towards the house. It was agreeable with him, cowboying for old Eli Henderson over in the Basin, but as a footloose rider he had no use at all for fifteen cows. "Let me talk it over with Miz' Drummond," he said to Eli Henderson. "If she's agreeable to gettin' back into the cow business, I'll sure take you up on your offer."

Henderson's tough old eyes turned sardonic again. He pulled at his moustache, ran his eyes up and down Sloan and seemed about to say something, which he never did say. He muttered, "Sure, sure, take your time." He then walked on up where young Trent was wiggling in among the Henderson riders up where the corralled mustangs were milling around scuffling up clouds of dust.

Young Matt said to Sloan: "You missed the fun out there at the trap. There are some scrappers in that horse-herd of yours."

"Not mine," stated Sloan, looking up there where young Trent was excitedly moving in and out among the cowboys. "Trent's horse-herd, Matt. Seems like a boy his age needs something to cut his teeth on."

Dougherty, silent up to now, looked squarely at Sloan. "You're goin' to give him a hand takin' the snap out of 'em, aren't you? Hell; a kid as green as that one can get hurt foolin' around mustangs unless he's got a pardner to steer him along."

Sloan nodded. "I figured to," he said, and turned as Matt touched his arm and jerked a thumb backwards.

Rita was down there by the well-box standing in mellow afternoon-shadows looking out where the dust was rising and the Henderson cowboys were hooting and laughing. Sloan turned and walked on down towards the house. As he came along Rita centred her attention upon him. She looked anxious.

"Is Trent all right?" she asked. "Those horses look

wild, Sloan."

"He'll be all right, ma'am. As for the horses—that's his start in life. Maybe it's not much but it's sure better than nothing." Sloan walked on over to the well-box, eased down with one leg dangling, singled out old Eli Henderson up among the riders lining the corral, and told Rita of the old cowman's proposition.

She heard him out, then said, "Yes; that's the same offer he made my husband. In fact that's how we acquired those thirty cows which were going to be the start of our herd."

"Well," said Sloan, still solemnly gazing far out. "I'm plumb willing to work it out with Henderson; only as a drifter, ma'am, I got no use at all for fifteen cows."

He swung his face towards her. She was watching him from the late-day shadows with a gentle, wondering expression. She didn't say anything so he spoke on, saying, "What I was thinkin', Rita, was that Trent could work into this salting and herding job along with breakin' his horses. It'd pretty well discipline him in the way life works out for a feller, if he's not lazy an' if he's honest with the feller he works for, as well as bein' honest with himself."

She still stood there softly watching his expression saying nothing, and when it seemed she never would speak, she said, "Can we talk about this later? I think the least we can do for the Henderson riders after all the help they've given us today, is feed them a big supper."

Sloan got up off the well-box and smiled over at her. "Sure; we can talk about it any time. And if I know cowboys, that bunch over there'll be your slaves for life if you give 'em a woman-cooked meal."

Rita smiled back at him. "Send Trent to me at the house, will you? I realise it's going to be a terrible come-down for him, having to work with a woman after spending the day among menfolk, but I'll need his help with the supper."

Sloan nodded and started away. He hadn't progressed more than a hundred feet towards the corrals when Rita called softly to him.

"Sloan; later on, after the men have gone back to their camp, I'd like to talk to you, if you're not too tired."

He considered her unsmiling but lovely face, nodded, and continued on towards the corrals. He had not said where he would be later on and she had not said where she would meet him; there was no need anyway. They had come together at other times out near the old pasture gate. It seemed a natural spot for a rendezvous.

He sauntered over where Eli Henderson stood with his riders appraising the horses. As an opener he said, "There are some in the bunch that ought to make fair-usin' cow horses."

Henderson turned, hung fire over his answer as he steadily studied Sloan, then he nodded. "Good bunch, Mister Verrill. Tell you what; when you get 'em broke and lined-out I'd like first crack at buyin' the best twenty head."

Sloan nodded. "I'll speak to Trent about it, Mister Henderson. It's a pardnership. And about that other proposition, if you still have in mind the same offer, we'll take it."

Henderson tugged at his droopy moustache. "Fine," he said, still closely watching Sloan. "I'll have the salt-wagon come up into the yard tomorrow and leave the salt bags. When we come back next fall to take the herd back home, you tell me which critters you've picked and we'll cut 'em out and corral 'em for you." Henderson shoved out his hand, he and Sloan shook, which was the rangeman's way of sealing a bargain, then, as Sloan swung and called Trent over, old Eli Henderson waited until the boy had been sent down to the house and well out of ear-shot before he said, "Mister Verrill, I make it a habit to keep my beak out'n other folkses affairs, an' I aim to do just exactly that between you an' Shelton Leonard. But you see, I know most of the boys who'll be ridin' in any posse he gets up from down at Bidwell, and since they won't know you, I been talkin' to my son and to Pat Dougherty. We decided to come up near the Pass for a day or two to sort of keep an eye on things. Our horses need the rest anyway, and I don't mind sayin' that at my age I got nothing against lyin' over a few days either."

Sloan regarded old Henderson's craggy, rough and scarred countenance for a while before speaking. He knew the kind of man old Henderson was; he never raised his voice nor ran a bluff, neither did he back off from trouble nor take one step forward in search of it. And finally, when he said he meant to wait around a few days to see what Shelton Leonard was up to, all the dissenting talk in the world would not change his mind one little bit, so Sloan simply lifted his shoulders and let them fall as he and the old cowman exchanged a long look.

Later, when Rita rang the supper bell and the cowboys turned with gleeful looks of anticipation towards the house, old Eli managed to be strolling down through the shadowy evening beside Sloan. For a hundred yards he just walked along looking solemn and saying nothing, but just short of the house he said, "You know, Mister Verrill, when a feller gets into his seventies he can say things a younger feller might get knocked on his duff for sayin'."

Sloan halted, half turned and waited. He thought he knew what was coming, and perhaps from anyone else it would have annoyed him, as old Eli had said, but now he felt no irritation at all.

Eli cocked his head upwards, ran the back of a hand under his Longhorn moustache and let the last of the men go on past into the house before he spoke, and then his voice was quiet and reminiscent.

"You know, Matt's mother died when he was ten years old. This here country is powerful hard on good women, Mister Verrill, powerful hard. Well; I raised him to the best of my lights."

"You did a good job, Mister Henderson."

Old Eli shrugged. "He's no better'n any other man an' no worse, Mister Verrill. But you know, raisin' a boy without a maw is damned hard. Damned hard. I'd say there'd be only one thing worse, Mister Verrill, an' that'd be raisin' a boy without any paw."

Sloan's hatbrim-shadowed eyes grew very still. He kept them steadily upon the tough old cowman there in the dusk with him, saying not a word.

"Now, I know what I told you a while back about makin' a habit of mindin' my own business. And I do; ask anyone who knows me, Mister Verrill. I do. I'm mindin' it right now, too, whether you think so or not. When I say you'n that boy belong together I'm thinkin' of my future herds over in Bitterbrush Basin—not you or the lad, particularly. It'd sure make me rest a heap easier if I knew every summer you'n your pardner'd be up here keepin' an eye on things for me—and of course buildin' up your own herd at the same time."

Sloan started to smile in spite of himself. Old Eli saw this and made a quick, hard scowl.

"Now I'm not suggestin' anything, mind you," he said quickly. "Because I make it a point to mind my own affairs. Still, Mister Verrill, if you were to— well—work something out an' stay in the country, it'd be a real blessing. A real blessing."

"The name," Sloan said slowly to that crafty old cowman, "is just plain Sloan. Not Mister Verrill."

"And I'm just plain Eli."

"Well, Eli, you're makin' a snap-judgment. I could

be as bad as Shelton Leonard for all you know about me."

"No," stated the old cowman, his faded eyes narrowing with shrewdness. "No you couldn't, Sloan. Like I said, I'm in my seventies. Lots of folks live that long and never learn a damned thing. I'm one of 'em. But one thing I *do* know is men, an' when a man as good with a gun as you are chose not to draw on Matthew, when you had reason to, and used a fist instead, you proved yourself my kind of a man. No, Sloan; my judgment in this case is plenty sound, an' if you can work out somethin' an' stay in this country, any time you need a friend—call on Eli Henderson. Now I reckon we'd better get inside or there won't be anything left."

Sloan went along beside Henderson as far as the door, held it open for the older man, and those two smiled into one another's eyes as they went on in out of the night.

SIXTEEN

ELI HENDERSON took his men out to their horses and back to their cow-camp a little short of nine o'clock. Every man among them was full of gratitude for the meal, and Rita had proved herself capable too; she'd baked four dried-apple pies along with everything else. Even Sloan was impressed with her ability. When she came strolling out where he stood in warm moonlight by the pasture gate an hour after the Henderson men had left, he told her for the second time how good that meal had been.

She smiled, gazing out over the star-washed land, and said, "I think perhaps too much flattery is worse than none at all."

"It wasn't meant for flattery," he said. "It was just the plain truth."

Her smile lingered. "That makes it much better, Sloan. It's been such a long time, too. . . ."

He took in a big breath, braced himself with both hands upon the gate and said, "I've been thinking, Rita. I guess I didn't arrive at any decision so much as the decision just sort of came along all by itself."

"Yes, Sloan?"

She was no longer smiling. Her expression was inward-seeming, withdrawn; she seemed suddenly to want him to speak while at the same time hoping that he wouldn't speak.

"Well. . . ."

A gunshot blew the hushed night apart. A blinding flash of crimson came down through the cottonwoods from the direction of the creek, but westward, up about where the dam was.

Sloan spun around, dropped down and drew his six-gun, all in one smooth movement. He had the blaze of muzzleblast to guide him as he thumbed off two rapid return-shots, got back another whistling slug and went flat down this time as that second bullet struck a tree-trunk with powerful force.

He tried another snap-shot at muzzleblast. He had

no other target. Then he waited for another answering slug. When none came he twisted to look back. Rita was lying crumpled twenty feet behind him. With a little strangled cry he dashed back, lifted her gently and sought the wound. That first bullet had struck her high in the chest, up near the collarbone. She was unconscious and freely bleeding.

With no further thought of caution Sloan put up his six-gun and trotted down towards the rear of the house with Rita in his arms. Once, as he passed across a spot of soft moonlight, that unseen rifleman snapped off another shot, but like the others this one also missed.

Just as Sloan got to the back door though, a gun erupted from off on his right, out upon the slope where that grave was, and this time the bullet seared into his flesh like hot iron. He gasped, staggered, recovered his balance and made it on into the house. It was dark as he limped on through the kitchen, but as he stepped into the parlour beyond a lamp flickered to life.

Young Trent was staring up at him from a white face and huge eyes. Sloan barked: "Put out that light!" Trent obeyed with alacrity and would have whimpered but Sloan said, "Lead the way to your mother's room, Trent, and be quick about it."

Trent padded swiftly along, led Sloan into a large, airy room on the south side of the house and stood back for Sloan to put his unconscious mother upon her own bed.

"See if there's still some water in the kettle on the stove," said Sloan. "If there is fetch it back in here along with a couple of towels and a basin. *Move!*"

Trent moved. He had no time to ask a question or cry. As soon as he left the room Sloan slipped the shoulder of Rita's dress down for a close examination of her wound. The bullet had fortunately been flying straight when it struck; if it had first ricocheted off a tree, had been tumbling end over end when it had struck, Rita Drummond would perhaps not have survived long enough to reach her own bed. As it now was, Sloan saw that the slug had gone completely through without actually touching a bone. Rita would be all right if she was kept still so no internal bleeding would begin.

He turned to examining his left leg where that bullet from the sidehill had come inward towards the rear of the house to make an angry welt across his calf, tear a six inch wide slit in his levis, and cause a painful cramp in his muscles. He was still examining this injury when young Trent returned, his eyes brim-full of hot, unshed tears.

Sloan took the basin, the pitcher of water, motioned for Trent to drag up a little bed-side table, put those objects down and held forth a hand for the clean towels Trent had also brought along.

"She'll be fine," he said to the lad. "Bullet went plumb through just under her shoulder. Knocked her out but she didn't even lose much blood. Step up closer here, son, I'm goin' to show you how to bandage a wound like this."

Sloan went to work cleansing the wound and wrapping it. As he worked he talked, pushed words out, sometimes not making a whole lot of sense, but quite succeeding in keeping young Trent so absorbed in what was being done to his mother the lad forgot all about whimpering.

When Sloan eventually finished, stood up and gingerly tested his own leg, he put a hand lightly upon the boy's shoulder. "Now you listen to me," he said. "I want you to sit right here beside her. When she comes around don't let her move. And no matter what you hear outside this house—don't you pay any attention to it. You stay right here an' make danged sure your mother's all right, you understand?"

"I understand," whispered troubled Trent Drummond. "Sloan? Who did it; who's out there tryin' to kill us?"

"Not us. Not you or your maw, son—me."

"But who—?"

"There are two of them, son. One's up the draw somewhere by the dam. In those aspens up there maybe. There's another one too; that one's west of the house up there by your paw's grave somewhere."

"Sloan, please don't go out there."

"Listen, pardner, we been attacked. One of us been hit. We didn't want any trouble, but now we're goin' to make a little." Sloan tested that cramp-muscled leg, found it not too averse to bearing his solid weight, and turned towards the bedroom door. As he started to pass on towards the yonder kitchen he called softly back, "Watch her very close, son, she's the best part of this pardnership we've got."

Beyond the house the night was ominously quiet. That slatternly old moon was up there with her diamond-bright variety of little stars casting an eerie brightness downward, but where the danger lay for Sloan Verrill cottonwood shadows closed out the light.

He got out of the house and ran southward to an edge of the building where he sprang around the corner and sank down waiting. But no shot came, the stillness ran on, there was no movement anywhere that he could determine.

Somewhere a long way off a man's abrupt yell echoed through the night. Sloan left his place of concealment at that sound, dashed recklessly for the pasture gate and made it without a shot being fired at him.

He trotted swiftly out through the cottonwoods until he had an uninterrupted view up that yonder slope where the grave lay gently sunken in front of its headboard, and tried hard to locate that second assassin out there.

He never did locate the man who had nearly shot him, though. Beyond any doubt that ambusher had fled at the first sound of riders coming swiftly down the night from the area of Tumbleweed Pass.

Sloan heard them coming and drew himself upright slowly, made sure there was no one up the slope, turned and started slowly back down towards the gate. He was confident that with the approach of Henderson's men in response to all that violent gunfire of minutes earlier, the pair of assassins had fled.

He stopped at the gate to punch out spent casings from his hand-gun and plug in fresh loads from his shell-belt. He was still engaged in this when Pat Dougherty, young Matt Henderson, and five more cowboys burst into the yard with their guns out and ready.

Sloan called forth, identifying himself, then moved out where the others could see him.

"What the hell happened?" yelled Dougherty. Then, seeing Sloan's slight limp Dougherty let off a bristling string of epithets and said, "Where are they; where are those two skulkin' 'breeds? By gawd I told Eli we'd ought to make our camp right here in this cussed yard tonight. Hey, Sloan; how bad's that leg; can you ride?"

"I can ride," stated Sloan, coming up abreast of Dougherty and young Matt. "But there's no time for catchin' horses an' saddlin 'em now, Pat. You and the others head west up. . . ."

"Frenchy," bawled bull-bass-voiced Pat Dougherty to one of the other Henderson riders. "Frenchy, give Sloan your horse. Hurry, dammit, we got to catch those two before they get back to Leonard's ranch."

A swarthy, moon-face cowboy hastily swung down, tossed Sloan his reins and jumped back as Sloan sprang for the saddle. Sloan twisted to look down at that unhorsed rider as Pat roared for them to dash away. "In the house," he called. "Frenchy, in the house. It's Miz Drummond—she's been hit. Do what you can for her."

Dougherty led the wild charge westward on up the draw. There were seven of them now, including Sloan Verrill. They did not spare their mounts either, not until, a half mile above the log-dam where the hillside became moderately steep, they had to slacken speed or run their animals out of wind.

But Dougherty cursed this delay. He had heard what Sloan had shouted back to Frenchy and the news that Rita Drummond had been shot seemed to spur wrathful Pat Dougherty to even greater efforts at overtaking the two bushwhacking gunmen.

It was a good night for a chase as Dougherty, young Matt Henderson and Sloan Verrill led the other Henderson riders up and over that westward rim and down the far side of it. Visibility was excellent, the weather was warm, and while none of them caught sight of Shelton Leonard's two 'breed cowboys, all of them were grimly convinced that was who it had been back there at the Drummond place, trying to kill Sloan Verrill.

There was some shouted conversation back and forth as the riders sped along, but mostly the men were silent until they'd struck the open country beyond that slope they'd just descended. Then Sloan Verrill called for a halt. As the horses came down to a fidgeting stand, all of them bunched up, Sloan called for silence.

The seven of them fought their horses to make them become quite still. It was not an easy thing; those animals had been run, but aside from that they'd been infected with some of the contagious excitement of their riders.

But after a while when the last horse ceased its stamping and moving, they all very clearly heard steel-shod hooves passing over far-away stone. Sloan said sharply: "West. They're still heading west."

Dougherty let off a sizzling oath and led out again with a slashing wave of his right arm. Around him the others swept along.

For almost an hour those seven riders went recklessly careening through and around stands of bitterbrush, sage and chapparal, until Sloan recognised the landswell dead ahead and slid his animal down to a halt behind it, at the same time calling upon the Henderson men to also halt.

As they came together again, Sloan dismounted, tugged out the Winchester under the fender of the saddle he was riding, levered it to make certain the weapon was loaded, then stepped on out where Dougherty and the others were following Sloan's example.

"On around this hill," said Sloan, "there lies about a mile and a half of open country before we get to the Leonard place. If my guess is correct, those two 'breeds will be holing up among the buildings down there, waiting for us."

"They asked for it," said Pat Dougherty. "Slippin' down in the night an' tryin' to assassinate you. What the hell moved 'em to do that anyway?"

"Cortez's funeral pyre," said Sloan. "You're forgettin' I spoiled Shelton Leonard's scheme, and when I spoiled it I also stored up some bad trouble for those two cowboys who were supposed to make sure nothin' happened while Leonard was gone."

"All right," snapped Dougherty, looking around as though anxious to get on over to the Leonard-ranch buildings. "But how in hell did they know. . . ?"

"Simple enough," broke in Sloan impatiently. "If you mean how did they know who I was, that's pretty simple, Pat. Only one man visited the Leonard place today—me. And I obviously was the feller who set fire to the shed where Cortez was being kept. Now it wouldn't take much of a brain to figure out I not only wasn't the deputy sheriff I made that cowboy think I was, but that I was the man Leonard had warned his two remaining men about."

Pat accepted this with a brusque nod. He stepped along towards the sloping shoulder of their shielding landswell, poked his head out and looked around. The others stepped quietly up and also looked out. They could not be seen in the moonlight from this distance, but neither could they see those two bushwhackers either, and at least one of the Henderson men was not enthusiastic about this. He kept looking around and muttering for the others to remember that men who'd once before slipped up and tried murder in the night were entirely capable of making a second attempt.

Sloan, who had most recently been over here, found now that in the night it was entirely possible for crouching men to approach within gun-range of the buildings; something he'd found totally impossible under the bright daytime sunlight.

"Come on," he said to the others, and led the way onward. The others followed him out into the moonlight to a man, and without any hesitation at all.

SEVENTEEN

T HEY got to the edge of the bitterbrush where it ended and brushed-off land began, halted there and crouched down. It had taken a half hour to get this far along without being seen but they had accomplished it. Ahead of them where ghostly moonlight lay across Shelton Leonard's old bleached ranch buildings, there was not a sound. Dougherty put his head over to Sloan and whispered.

"They didn't ride on past or we'd have heard 'em, so they got to be over there."

Sloan nodded. He could understand Dougherty's misgivings, but at the same time he knew positively those two bushwhackers were among the yonder buildings. "Split up," he said. "Pat; take two men and slip plumb around and come in behind the buildings. Matt; keep one rider here with you so they can't make a break for it back the way they came. I'll take one feller and head on around to the north." Sloan poked a finger at a snub-nosed, freckled cowboy and jerked his head. As those two started crawling away Sloan said, "Don't shoot unless you have to. I'd like to get at least one of these beauties alive as witness against Leonard."

The night was utterly still. There were horses in the barn, Sloan heard them make little sounds, but aside from that there was nothing to be heard until, just as Sloan and his companion dropped flat-down to confer, a gun exploded from over by Shelton Leonard's barn, the flash was visibly southward. Sloan's companion said sharply, "Saw somethin' down there; maybe Pat or someone else movin' through the brush."

Sloan made no comment. He eased up just a little, pushed his six-gun over a buckbrush plant and snapped off a return-shot in the direction of that rifleman down in the yard.

This triggered the battle; at once two carbines lanced red flame northward as Sloan and his companion pressed flat against the ground.

From out where Matt was, two more guns opened up, and finally, from southward, down where Pat Dougherty and his pardner were, came more flashes of searing gunfire.

The freckle-faced cowboy squinted over at Sloan and said, "That ought to convince those 'breeds they're surrounded."

Sloan nodded, but he wasn't at all enthusiastic about how this fight might end. The cowboys over among Leonard's ranch buildings at least had shelter, while the men with Sloan had nothing but the star-washed night and some spindly clumps of brush to hide behind.

For a full minute the surrounding riders poured lead in among the buildings. From time to time one of

Leonard's men fired back, but evidently they were more concerned with lying low than with trying to fight their way clear of the surround, because even when they fired it did not seem to Sloan that they were concentrating upon any particular targets.

When a lull came, Sloan yelled out to the beseiged men. "You're in a pocket," he called. "You can't possibly fight clear. If you're smart you'll throw down those guns."

Instead of a verbal answer Sloan got four fast shots thrown in the direction of his voice. The cowboy with him swore with feeling as one of those bullets cut brush not ten feet from where he lay.

"Never mind doin' that again," the cowboy said to Sloan. "Givin' them fellers a chance is about like makin' friends with a pair of wolves."

Sloan remained quiet for as long as it took him to make a careful ground-level study of the onward buildings, work out a way to get in closer and start crawling forward. Behind him the Henderson rider got up on to all fours and followed along, but he kept his head moving from side to side as he crept along.

The pair of them got half way around to where Leonard's old barn partially shielded them, when a furious exchange of gunfire broke out between Dougherty and the man with him, and the two men in the ranch yard. For as long as it took Sloan to figure out that none of this lead was coming his way, he and his companion lay belly-down, but afterwards, when they were satisfied the 'breed riders in among the buildings were facing away from them, Sloan sprang up, said, "Come on," and made a reckless dash for the nearby corrals.

They got safely over where corral-shadows lay thickly criss-crossing one another, paused to briefly catch their breath, then went ducking through corral stringers until, within twenty feet of the yonder barn, that angry firing around the barn somewhere southward, suddenly ended. Then they halted.

The cowboy stuck his face close and whispered. "If Leonard's gunnies don't get us now it's a pretty good chance Pat or Matt or someone out beyond the yard darned well might do it for them, if they see us movin' down here."

Sloan had already thought of that. He nodded, but instead of answering, he pointed to the rear of the barn where a gloomy, big, dark opening loomed. The pair of them started inching their way towards that opening. They were within fifty feet of it gliding along the rear wall of the building, when around the far corner a tall shadow appeared. Evidently, after that last wrathful exchange, at least one of Shelton Leonard's men had the same idea about getting inside the barn for protection.

Sloan spotted their enemy a second ahead of being spotted himself. He grunted and dropped like a stone, rolled and snapped off a shot which missed but which alerted the 'breed that he was not alone around here. As Leonard's man sprang back he also fired and missed.

The freckle-faced cowboy swore and got off two rapid shots, one of which sang off overhead while the other one slammed into barn-siding with a slashing, tearing sound.

That 'breed got safely back around the barn's corner and bleated to his pardner that their enemies were in the yard with them. At once, from southward and out where a few little winking red embers still glowed from that burnt-out shed Sloan had set afire hours earlier, came a ground-sluicing carbine shot. Sloan winced and rolled frantically forward as lead splintered wood close to him. Behind him the freckle-faced cowboy fired once and tried to fire a second time; Sloan heard the firing-pin drop upon a spent casing. Until his companion could re-load the fight was now exclusively between Leonard's two riders and Sloan. He tried to recall how many slugs he had left, couldn't, and stretched out flat in barn-shadows, lay his six-gun over his left forearm and waited.

It was not a long wait. The cowboy out by the gutted shed levered his carbine, fired, sprang up and raced wildly for the corner of the barn where his pardner was. Sloan tracked him, lightly squeezed the trigger, and five feet from safety the 'breed gave a high bound into the air, flung his Winchester violently away, and crumpled.

Sloan immediately swung his attention to the corner of the barn expecting the remaining 'breed cowboy to spring forth and fire. But the surviving man did not do this; he did not fire at all.

Behind Sloan his companion was furiously re-loading. He was also helplessly swearing as he did this, each word falling breathlessly into the settling silence. Sloan drew both legs up, got them under him and flung his head around. "Run for it," he hissed, and whipped fully upright as he lunged off to the left in the direction of that inviting, doorless barn opening.

He made it, sprang over the threshold into stygian darkness, and twisted to see how his companion was doing. From eastward out over the yard two six-guns roared in their thunderous fashion. Southward too, another pair of .45s erupted. Lead hit the barn from several different directions just as Sloan's companion came racing in out of the ghostly night, his breathing raspingly loud.

For as long as those Henderson men beyond the yard kept up their probing gunfire neither Sloan nor his pardner moved. It was black inside the barn, neither of them could see five feet around in any direction, and it was in both their minds that since the surviving 'breed cowboy had been also trying to get inside, they had better remain completely silent and motionless just in case the 'breed had succeeded.

Pat Dougherty's bull-bass voice rose up out of the southward night calling for Leonard's riders to surrender and promising, that if they did not surrender at once, when the Henderson men finally took them, Pat would personally furnish the lariat and the strong right arm to hang them both from Shelton Leonard's own barn baulk.

Sloan and the freckle-faced cowboy stood absolutely still for as long as it took for Leonard's surviving rider to make his decision, and when the freckle-faced rider looked around, his face nothing more than a white blob in the darkness, Sloan whispered: "Quiet; he's got no choice and by now he knows it. We're inside his barn, the others, for all he knows right now, are also closin' in on him, and he's got his pardner's dead body to demoralise him out there. Be quiet and wait. If he's goin' to answer at all it'll be pretty quick now."

It was "pretty quick." The 'breed called forth in response to Pat's demand in a rough, sullen voice. "I quit, you fellers. I'm leavin' my guns here beside the barn. I got enough."

Dougherty said, "How about your friend; he got enough too?"

"He's dead," said that same rough voice. "There's two of your friends inside the barn here. One of 'em got him. What you want me to do?"

"Walk out into the centre of the yard," came back Dougherty's sharp reply. "Keep your paws over your danged head and don't move after you're out in the middle of the yard."

Sloan heard the 'breed finally move; he had been exactly where Sloan had last seen him, around the corner of the barn.

The freckle-faced rider touched Sloan's sleeve and started tip-toeing forward through the barn towards the doorless front opening where he'd have a good

163

view of their prisoner when the 'breed emerged into the yard. Sloan followed him forward. They both halted back in gloomy shadows where they had an excellent onward view, and waited.

The 'breed cowboy came into sight from alongside the barn, hesitated to cast a worried look around, then stepped forth out into the yard, marched twenty feet ahead with both arms high, then halted.

Sloan and his companion stepped out of the barn, put up their weapons and called forth to the other Henderson men that it was now safe to leave shelter.

Matt Henderson was the first one to hasten up. The second man was Pat Dougherty, still carrying his cocked carbine and swinging his head from left to right as though unconvinced that other 'breed was truly dead. Gradually, the rest of the attackers came out of the night and grimly, silently, gathered around the captive.

Sloan said, "Pat; he wasn't lyin'. I downed the other one out behind the barn." Then Sloan went over to look into the face of their prisoner. It was the same lanky, dark cowboy he'd fooled into thinking he was a lawman much earlier. He and the 'breed exchanged a long, flinty stare, then Sloan said, "Which one were you—the one up by Drummond's log dam, or the one up the sagebrush slope near the grave?"

The 'breed, his eyes dark with rancour, said, "The one up the slope hidin' behind that headboard. What of it?"

"Nothing much," drawled Sloan. "But if you'd been

the one up by the dam you'd die right here, because that one shot Miz' Drummond."

Matt Henderson said harshly, "How do we know he wasn't the one who did it, anyway? He'd lie to save his neck."

"We know," explained Sloan, "because neither of them could've known they'd hit her, so he wouldn't know he had to lie."

Pat Dougherty eased off the hammer of his carbine, grounded the weapon and leaned upon it staring at the 'breed. "What made you take that chance?" he asked. "You couldn't have helped but know the rest of us were camped up by Tumbleweed Pass and would hear the shootin'."

"We had to," growled the lanky 'breed, his face sulky and vicious. "This here feller burnt the shack down with Cortez's body in it. He destroyed Mister Leonard's evidence."

"Evidence hell," growled Sloan. "You know dog-gone well those two bullets were pumped into Cortez's back after he was dead."

"The law wouldn't have known that though," said the 'breed, giving Sloan glare for glare. "An' that's what Mister Leonard was countin' on to get even with you with; that back-shot corpse. But you had to come over here and destroy everythin'. So Frank Cosineau an' I talked it over; we come to the conclusion the only way to keep from bein' in bad trouble with Mister Leonard, was for us to sneak down to the Drummond place and bushwhack you. After all, that's what Mister

Leonard wanted—you dead—an' how it got done wouldn't make no difference to him, just so long as it was done."

The Henderson riders gazed around at one another. One of them shook his head in solemn condemnation, saying, "Listen, fellers; what's the point of takin' him on back to the Drummond place? Why not just string him up right here an' have done with it?"

The others were beginning to mutter assent when Pat Dougherty said, "You bunch of idiots; this here feller's going to give the evidence against Shelton Leonard we've been waitin' almost twenty years for someone to come up with. If we hang him, Leonard'll lie his way clear sure as the devil."

The riders subsided and turned to thoughtfully consider the big 'breed. One of them said, "Pat; what proof we got he won't make up a big story too?"

"There are seven of us," said Sloan Verrill, "who heard every word he just said, so he can lie until he gets blue in the face and it won't change a cussed thing. Come on; let's get back astride and head for home. I want to know how Miz' Drummond is."

They got a horse for their prisoner, tied him upon it, went after their own animals and started the return trip. From time to time someone would speak, but mostly they rode along in silence. They left the dead 'breed gunman, Frank Cosineau, back there behind the barn where he had died.

EIGHTEEN

T HEY got back to the Drummond place in the small hours of the morning. The Henderson riders found old Eli awaiting them over at the house, along with several others including young Trent. As Sloan swung down and started for the house old Eli Henderson called to him.

"She's finally asleep, an' I reckon she needs sleep right now about as much as she needs anything, so maybe you could put off visitin' her for a spell."

"Sure," said Sloan, pacing back over beside the old cowman. "How is she?"

"Fine," replied old Eli. "As good as folks can be with a bullet-hole through 'em. But it was a clean wound and you did a right fine job of patchin'. She'll be all right 'thin a few days."

Trent came up and stood beside Sloan gazing up at him. "Mister Henderson says if you hadn't bandaged maw just right, Sloan, she might've bled real bad."

Sloan cocked a sceptical eye at the old cowman and Eli Henderson said swiftly and defensively, "Well now, it could've happened. I've seen folks bleed out real bad from. . . ."

"Not that little puncture an' you know it," said Sloan.

Henderson fidgeted, lowered his voice and said, "It never hurt a lad to think some particular man was ten feet tall. Never hurt 'em a bit."

Pat Dougherty came over accompanied by Matt Henderson. Matt had a cup of coffee and Dougherty had two cups, one of which he handed across to Sloan. "Locked the 'breed in the barn," he said, and looked down at young Trent. "How's your mother, boy?"

"Mister Henderson says she'll be fine in a day or two," Trent replied, turned and said, "Sloan; tell me what happened over there; did you. . . ?"

"You," said Sloan cutting in, "go put up my horse and see if you can't help the other fellers with their animals. An' when you're through there, go pitch a few flakes of hay out to the mustangs. By then it'll be sunup, an' you can go lay a fire in the kitchen stove for breakfast."

Trent made a face. The cowboys standing around laughed and cat-called after the boy as he walked away. Old Eli Henderson eyed Sloan a moment, then started over towards the barn where an armed cowboy sat outside the door guarding the captive inside. Old Eli went on in and was gone for a great while talking to Shelton Leonard's cowboy. In fact, by the time he returned to the yard, off in the dim east there was a faint blush of pre-dawn light. He went directly over where Sloan, Pat Dougherty and young Matt Henderson were talking, and said, "That one's name is Turtle Shaughnessy. He told me some interestin' things. For example; those thirty cows Leonard stole from Mrs. Drummond, Shelton Leonard drove over to Bidwell an' sold to the town butcher over there."

Matthew gazed at his father. "I can guess what you

got in mind," he said.

Old Eli's tough gaze kindled with indignation. "Well now, son, Leonard ran those cattle last year, an' since they were all bred cows and would've calved, why I calculate Shelton Leonard owes the widow Drummond thirty cows and thirty yearlings."

"Paw," said young Matt solemnly, "there'd be this spring's calves too."

Eli bobbed his head up and down. "Another thirty head," he said. "Tell you what we ought to do while we're standin' around here this mornin'. We ought to go ride. . . ."

"Riders comin'," bawled a man out front by the hitchrack. "Looks like at least ten of 'em an' they're comin' fast."

At once all the Henderson men moved off towards the front of the house. Sloan turned, saw that armed guard up by the barn, and called back to him.

"Fetch the prisoner along too. Keep his arms tied behind him an' don't let him make a sound."

The sun was not quite visible off in the east but its initial glow stood straight up from below the horizon brightening the world to a soft, watery grey. Visibility was good close by, but not at a distance, so all those watching men, while they could make out the oncoming riders, could not make out who they were. Not until, out a half mile, the riders slowed and one of them called back over his shoulder for the others to watch carefully from here on. Then those silent, motionless cowboys recognised the voice of Shelton

Leonard and turned to gaze over where Sloan Verrill was standing between the two Hendersons with big, rough Pat Dougherty standing farther back.

The oncoming men, evidently guided to the Drummond place by a solitary lamp burning in Rita's bedroom, slowed to a walk and kept right on moving up. They did not see all those quiet-standing armed men until they were practically to the house itself.

Shelton Leonard was in the lead riding a tucked-up big grulla horse who seemed pushed to his very limit. He walked along mechanically, his head hanging and his footsteps shuffling from weariness.

Sloan stepped forth as soon as Leonard yanked back at sight of all those grim, still faces lining the front of the house.

"Get down," Sloan said. "Leonard, get down!"

Leonard swung towards that voice, his head whipping around with full recognition. Behind him the men he'd brought from Bidwell jammed up close and also halted. Several of them dropped right hands to gun-butts and sat like that, obviously not expecting the powerful number of men awaiting them and not quite clear as to just what they should do about this now.

They did nothing; all along the front of the house men began cocking exposed guns. No matter how good those horsemen from Bidwell were, they couldn't possibly compete with guns which were already drawn and cocked.

Sloan took five long steps, halted beside Leonard's

head-hung grulla horse and glared. "I said get down and I meant it. *Leonard, dismount!*"

Leonard did. He swung out and down, lit with both booted feet close set, and threw a vicious punch which caught Sloan high on the cheek and nearly put him down. He staggered away shaking his head. Around him Dougherty, Matt, even old Eli Henderson roared with indignation and moved in with their drawn guns.

Sloan barked at them: "Keep out of it. Stay back."

The Henderson men altered course, moved in among the riders Leonard had returned from Bidwell with, and disarmed these strangers then yanked them down to stand beside their mounts.

Sloan's head cleared; he stepped right, stepped left, and when Shelton Leonard fired twice in both those directions and missed with each fist, Sloan stopped bobbing, stopped weaving, feinted Leonard in close, got under his guard and straightened up with a powerful left, a lethal right, crossed over with the sledging left again, and caught Leonard as he sagged, slapped him hard on both cheeks with an open hand and shoved him off. Leonard stumbled backwards, fell, and sat there rolling his head and gasping. For the second time he had been bludgeoned into submission by the same granite fists.

Eli Henderson strolled forward, bent from the waist to gaze upon Leonard, and straightened up to say to one of his men: "Fetch that 'breed around here."

When the prisoner was produced Eli caught Shelton Leonard by the shoulder, hauled him to his feet and pushed him over where he had a good view of the captive. "See that cowboy," said old man Henderson to Shelton Leonard, "Well, sir, he told us quite a bit about you; about shootin' slugs into a dead man from behind, about stealin' Miz' Drummond's cows, an' some other things too—like tryin' to get Sloan Verrill hanged. Now, Leonard, I'm goin' to see that you go to prison for these things, but first I want you to explain to these here boys you hired down in Bidwell just what kind of an illegal fight you came 'thin an ace of leadin' them into."

Shelton Leonard looked dazedly around. He looked longest at his 'breed cowboy standing over there with both arms tied behind him.

"Listen," he said in a voice so low Sloan and Eli Henderson had to strain to hear it. "Listen; I'll give back her cows."

"How can you?" asked old Eli. "They got butchered over in town last year."

Leonard gave his bound cowboy a fiery glare. "All right; I'll give her replacements. I'll give her thirty cows and. . . ."

"Thirty," roared big rough Pat Dougherty. "Why, damn you, Leonard, those cows were bred an' had calves by their sides when you rustled 'em. An' last year they'd have had more calves. By my figures you owe Miz' Drummond ninety head."

"Ninety head!" roared Shelton Leonard, looking wild-eyed at the wooden faces around him. "Ninety head! Are you out of your mind?"

Dougherty strode over, yanked down a lariat from one of the saddles of the men from Bidwell, rolled out a little calf loop, and as he passed back over the yard he casually flicked the loop over Shelton Leonard's head, snugged up the slack and said to the cowboys standing close by, "Lend a hand, friends; over to the nearest cottonwood with him. I was gettin' tired of all this talkin' anyway. Besides, it's near breakfast time."

At once half a dozen cowboys rushed over and laid hands upon Dougherty's rope. Leonard squealed, he set his feet and would have raised both hands to cast off the rope, but Sloan said, "Leave it on. You take it off and I'll break your jaw, Leonard."

The rope stayed on but Shelton Leonard began bleating. He swore Sloan could pick out any ninety head he wished from the Leonard herds. He promised to pay for damages, said he'd even leave the country, if his captors just would not lynch him.

Those riders he'd brought from Bidwell looked ashamedly at one another and on around at the Henderson men. One of them said to Sloan, "Hell; the way he explained it to us there was this mad-dog killer up here pot-shootin' folks in the back, and he'd pay five hundred to any feller who'd down this feller. We sure never had any idea things would turn out to be so plumb different, or mister, we'd nary a one of us have ridden out here with him."

Old Eli was talking to Leonard now and Sloan, as disgusted as the men from Bidwell also were, walked on over where Pat Dougherty was standing with a bitter sneer across his face.

When Sloan came up Dougherty said, "Doesn't that beat all? Fair turns my stomach listenin' to that yellow dog whine and bleat like that."

Sloan turned at the soft sound of his name being spoken from over by the house. Rita was standing over there supporting herself upon young Trent's arm. She had what seemed to be a big blue army overcoat across her shoulders and one arm was hanging in a sling. He crossed over, mounted the steps and halted there, looking worried. "You got no business being out here," he said. "Trent; what the devil'd you fetch her out here for? She's got to stay in bed for at least. . . ."

"Sloan," Rita said, speaking too quietly for the others out there in the dawn-lighted yard to hear. "I had to come out. Eli told me where you'd gone. I had to come out when Trent told me you were back. I wanted to be certain you weren't hurt."

"Hurt?" said Sloan. "I wasn't even close to gettin'. . . ."

"And to ask you to finish what you started to say just before that first shot sounded tonight, when you and I were standing up there by the pasture gate."

Sloan looked blank. It took him almost a full minute to find the threads of that much earlier conversation, and although he recalled what he'd had in mind with no difficulty, he could not now recall the exact words he'd had in mind, so he stood there looking dumbly over at her, saying nothing.

Out in the yard where all those men stood, for the most part with their backs to the front of the house, voices droned on, sometimes rising, sometimes dropping. The most noticeable voice belonged to Shelton Leonard. He had been told he was going back to Bidwell to stand trial for rustling, for conspiring to commit murder, and for a whole catalogue of crimes Henderson's riders invented as they stood around him, and he was pleading for mercy at the same time he was offering cash or cattle to anyone who would help him. No one offered to help him, so he kept on bleating, imploring, beseeching, his voice going on and on while Sloan tried to frame up the words to cover how he felt towards beautiful Rita Drummond.

"It had to do with gettin' married," Sloan said with a ring of triumph in his voice. "I remember now, Miss Rita; it had to do with. . . ."

"But who, Sloan?" Rita asked. "Who was going to get married?"

"Why danged it all, ma'am—you'n I."

Sloan had no sooner made that quite matter-of-fact statement than its full import struck him. He put forth a steadying hand upon the porch railing and stared. Rita smiled. She stepped over and lifted her face to him. He dropped his head, met her lips, and wasn't at all conscious of the abrupt, endless silence until he raised his head and saw all those wooden faces out there staring reproachfully up at him.

"The least you could've done," said rough Pat Dougherty, "was take her inside the cussed house; after all, Sloan Verrill, she's the prettiest—and onliest—woman for sixty miles around and there isn't

175

a rider here this mornin' who hasn't at one time or another been plumb desperate in love with the Widder Drummond. Then you come ridin' along and. . . ." Pat lifted his big shoulders, let them fall, and turned his back on Sloan.

Eli chuckled, doffed his hat and gallantly bowed low from the waist. "Knew it'd finish up like this," he said. "Fine lookin' woman, fine lookin' man—it just plain had to, didn't it, Trent?"

The lad stood there alternately blushing and looking as pleased as any boy could look who had just acquired a father as well as a pardner.

Center Point Publishing
600 Brooks Road • PO Box 1
Thorndike ME 04986-0001 USA

(207) 568-3717

US & Canada:
1 800 929-9108